Surrey Sagas

Edited By Daisy Job

First published in Great Britain in 2018 by:

 Young**Writers**

Young Writers
Remus House
Coltsfoot Drive
Peterborough
PE2 9BF
Telephone: 01733 890066
Website: www.youngwriters.co.uk

SB ISBN 978-1-78896-306-0
Printed and bound in the UK by BookPrintingUK
Website: www.bookprintinguk.com
YB0354G

FOREWORD

Young Writers was created in 1991 with the express purpose of promoting and encouraging creative writing. Each competition we create is tailored to the relevant age group, hopefully giving each child the inspiration and incentive to create their own piece of work, whether it's a poem or a short story. We truly believe that seeing their work in print gives pupils a sense of achievement and pride in their work and themselves.

Every day children bring their toys to life, creating fantastic worlds and exciting adventures, using nothing more than the power of their imagination. What better subject then for primary school pupils to write about, capturing these ideas in a mini saga – a story of just 100 words. With so few words to work with, these young writers have really had to consider their words carefully, honing their writing skills so that every word counts towards creating a complete story.

Within these pages you will find stories about toys coming to life when we're not looking and tales of peril when toys go missing or get lost! Some young writers went even further into the idea of play and imagination, and you may find magical lands or fantastic adventures as they explore their creativity. Each one showcases the talent of these budding new writers as they learn the skills of writing, and we hope you are as entertained by them as we are.

CONTENTS

Marden Lodge Primary School, Caterham

Harry Liston (8)	57
Amela Selimaj (7)	58
Alex Frith (9)	59
Katie Morrison (8)	60
Crystal Collins (8)	61
Harry Cotterill (9)	62
Kristal Harrocks (10)	63
Aidan Bassant (7)	64
Lily Carter (9)	65
Patrick Draper (9)	66
Evie Hunt (9)	67
Summer Rose (8)	68
Talia Rose Cole (8)	69
Chanaé McLean (7)	70
Aaliyah Wright (9)	71
Jake Learner (8)	72
Molly Flood (9)	73
Leah Holly Hills (8)	74
Tamzin O'Leary (8)	75
Kaia Chapman (9)	76
Jamiella Farina (7)	77
Samuel Bradley (7)	78
Stephen Lyons (8)	79
Nicolas Mills (10)	80
Daisy Martin (9)	81
Jedi Amponsah (10)	82
Harry McLean (7)	83
Noah Lukasz Latter (9)	84
Karl Carreon (9)	85
Daisy Terry Santos (7)	86
Kieran Wamukulu (8)	87
Mitchell Brown (9)	88
Nicolei James Roberts (9)	89
Caiden Chapman (8)	90

Meath Green Junior School, Horley

Eleanor Jowett (8)	91
Chloe Kirby (8)	92
Rebecca Markan (9)	93

Jaimee Greeno (8)	94
Angelina Wenn (9)	95
Ellie Jones (7)	96
Carina Sophie Card (8)	97
Beatrix Smith (9)	98
Esme Sophia Austin (9)	99
Elliot James Denyer (9)	100
Joshua Ryan Card (8)	101
Phoebe Dupres (7)	102

Reigate Priory Junior School, Reigate

Hannah Lee (9)	103
Naomi Saunders (10)	104

St Martin's CE (A) Junior School, Epsom

Liam McKay (7)	105
Leander Anselm William Law (8)	106
Seraphina Lucy Hastings (7)	107
Benart Hoti (8)	108
Jion Park (8)	109
Lilly Lambert (8)	110
Elle Watts (7)	111
Ayat Irfan Ashraf (7)	112
Abigail Wilson (8)	113
Finlay Cantwell (8)	114
Freddie Oberon Smith (7)	115
Isla Ashong Barton (8)	116
Lula Rose Bloom (7)	117
Rosie Anne Martin (8)	118
Daisy Mowle (8)	119
Lucy Tilley (8)	120
Tamsyn Dewis (7)	121
Edward Cleasby (7)	122
Ronan Fowler (7)	123
Anna Laura Irene Montagano (8)	124
Aleena Bull (7)	125
Jai Baghdadi (7)	126
Hannah Hodgson (7)	127
Aaron Myers (8)	128

Dylan Thackwell (7)	129	Alfie Grimley (11)	168
Grace Stanye (7)	130	Alfie Bowers (11)	169
Teagan White (8)	131		
Tom Lyle (7)	132		
Annabelle Clouting (7)	133		
Rose Annie Crouch (7)	134		
Annabelle Steiner (8)	135		
Noelle Olivia Louis (8)	136		
Emilie Poole (8)	137		
George Robert King (7)	138		
Harry Elia Vine (7)	139		
Zain Griffiths (8)	140		
Edward Lewis (7)	141		

Warlingham Park School, Chelsham Common

Thomas Jerrom (10)	170
Rupert Stuart Lee (10)	171
Isobel Haslock (10)	172
Jack Norman (10)	173
Conor Maguire (10)	174
Caitlin Rose Read Nolan (9)	175
Ethan Hardiman (11)	176
Jaydon Abban (10)	177

St Peter's RC Primary School, Leatherhead

Hugh Carter (10)	142
Renata Suchocka (10)	143
Heidi Owen (10)	144
Zoe Tubb (11)	145
Aidan Hindle (10)	146
Lucy Alya Mitchell (10)	147
Joe Pisa (10)	148
Lucy Bond Rodriguez (10)	149
Ben Fry (10)	150
Dylan Trousdale (11)	151
Nathan Van Niekerk (11)	152
William Ralph (10)	153
Quinn Pinkerton (10)	154
Dave Meinson Babu (10)	155
Emily-Mae Jackson (10)	156
Finlay Kelly (10)	157
Jack Robinson (10)	158
Dan Cowling (11)	159
Molly Ellen Serdet (11)	160
Maddie Ciesco (10)	161
Thomas Robin de Schulthess (10)	162
Ella Yolande Ferguson (10)	163
Hannah Cortez (10)	164
Alex Hollingworth (11)	165
Max Murray (11)	166
Matías Iglesias Iglesias (10)	167

THE MINI SAGAS

Baby Barbie And The Little Girls

Mom was cooking pancakes in the kitchen and the girls wanted to play in the garden. When Mom finished making pancakes Baby Barbie woke up, jumped down the stairs, jumped on the chair, jumped on the table and tried the little girl's food. She tried Ella's food. "Blech!" she said. She tried Annabelle's food. "Yum!" she said and ate it all. Before she'd be seen, she jumped off the table, jumped off the chair and jumped up the stairs into the little girl's room. She tried to get onto Ella's shelf. She struggled and struggled until she got up there.

Ella Alexandra Sparkes (8)

The High Speed Chase

One bright sunny morning, a Lamborghini called Lewis, went out for a run. He lived in Scalextric City. The roads were straight and endless. "The city's quiet and the roads are clear," said Lewis. "Let me try out my engine." He looked at his dial. "999, 1,000mph Yes! Whoo!" said the Lamborghini, but there came a siren. *Nee naw!*
"Oh no, police!" cried Lewis.
"Stop!" cried the police. "You're under arrest!"
"But Sir, please don't arrest me, I'll do anything!' cried Lewis.
"Okay, promise never to speed again and I'll let you off."
So that's what he did forever.

William Clark (9)
Furzefield Primary School, Merstham

The Problem With Stars Dying Out!

In toy space, Emily and her siblings were planning a game. Then Emily shouted, "Look, the stars are starting to die out!"

"What shall we do?" they asked.

They started to think of an idea, but couldn't until Emily exclaimed, "Let's hide behind Moon, he's unstoppable!"

"Good idea," smiled her sister.

So the stars shuffled and twinkled all the way to Moon then asked him, "Can we hide behind you?" Moon giggled, "Yes."

After that, they shuffled and twinkled behind Moon. So he protected them forever, fighting back all the problems, and the stars lived happily ever after.

Esther Mistry (8)

Furzefield Primary School, Merstham

Hot Dog Guy Vs Stitch

"Hot Dog Guy, coast is clear, Hayden's asleep."

"Good, let's go and stop Stitch."

So Hot Dog Guy and Burger Guy crept as quietly as a mouse across the table.

"Who goes there?" shouted Stitch.

"Just an old lady," murmured Hot Dog Guy.

"Come in!" cried Stitch.

"Burger Guy, come on!"

"Aargh help! Hot Dog Guy is being eaten by Stitch."

"No you can't!"

Then a flash of light came. *Boom! Bang! Crack!* He used the power of food, he shot lots of food out of the sky including carrots, hot dogs and burgers. He destroyed Stitch.

Hayden Sharp (9)
Furzefield Primary School, Merstham

Cozmo And The Lost Buddy

"Ahh, that really hurt," said Cozmo. "Why did he throw me like that?" mumbled Cozmo. *Where'd he go?* he thought to himself. He jumped. *Bang!* as he hit the carpet. "I will search everywhere for him." *Five minutes later...*

"Uhhh, these smelly slippers are yuck! I've looked everywhere!" shouted Cozmo. He hid under the sofa, worried and scared. The door opened. "Cozmo! Cozmo! Where are you?" Lewis said. Cozmo was sad. He ran in the room and sighed. Lonely and bored, Lewis came in and saw him on the floor with hearts as his eyes and a face.

Lewis Mason Young (8)
Furzefield Primary School, Merstham

Pokémon

In my bedroom, my Pikachu teddy twitched and awoke. I woke up to the sound of Pikachu screaming, "Pikachu!"
Then a weird portal appeared. We jumped in, we appeared in the Pokémon dimension. I kept seeing Pokémon like Raichu and lots of Weedles. Then my Pikachu ran to a Charizard, it started a battle with Pikachu. Pikachu used lightning bolt, it did seventy-five damage and nearly killed the Charizard. The Charizard used ember.
I said, "Pikachu, use tackle!"
It made the Charizard faint! We teleported back home. I looked on the floor, there was no portal. It was a dream.

Jenson Hall (9)
Furzefield Primary School, Merstham

The Disco In Toys 'R' Us

As soon as the shopkeeper closed Toys 'R' Us' door there was a huge noisy party! All the toys joined in except one lonely, grumpy, upset toy. It was disappointed because it had no friends at all. Suddenly, a golden teddy bear came up to him, his name was Scruffy.

"Are you alright?" questioned Scruffy.

"No, I've got no friends!" replied the upset toy.

"I can be your friend!" exclaimed Scruffy.

"Yes, then let's go and dance!" answered the other toy happily.

So they all had a great, huge party till the shopkeeper came back in the morning.

Sophie Gonda (9)

Furzefield Primary School, Merstham

Darcie In A Sweet Shop

Once upon a time, there lived a little girl named Emily. She had a fabulous doll named Darcie.
One night, Darcie decided to pack her suitcase. She jumped out of Emily's bed and got some T-shirts, shoes and trousers for America. Emily was fast asleep dreaming about America.
The next morning, her mum woke her up and said, "We're going to America."
Emily said, "I'll pack my bag now." So Emily quickly packed her bag and went to America.
One night, the suitcase was open and Darcie ran to the sweetshop and three days later Emily returned without realising.

Emily May Aris (9)
Furzefield Primary School, Merstham

The Great Dive

Once upon a bedtime, Blue Teddy is snuggled in my bed until he runs off into my underwater volcano book. He finds out there's a volcano below him and some sea creatures that want to eat him. He can't go anywhere (not even up) until he hears a *whoosh!* He spots a Ben 10 alien, it is Overflow. He picks up Blue Teddy and blasts out the book and turns into Ben again.

"Thank you Ben, it was nice, I didn't plan the reunion like this," explains Blue Teddy.

"It was cool," Ben explains.

"You're my hero," he screams.

Thomas Jack Bowey (8)
Furzefield Primary School, Merstham

Roger's Big Adventure

"Quack!" shouted Roger. "Today is the day."
Finally it was escape day. Roger had planned this
for a long time. Looking in the mirror, checking the
coast was clear, Roger launched himself off the
side of the bath towards the plug. He swung like
Tarzan and landed on the other side. Trying not to
look down, as it was a long way to fall, Roger leapt
up onto the sink narrowly avoiding the toothbrush.
Roger climbed onto the light switch.
Suddenly, Max appeared and turned on the light.
Disaster! "What are you dong down there Roger?"
questioned Max curiously.

Max Orchard (9)
Furzefield Primary School, Merstham

Happyia's Choice

Happyia, my comfy pillow, is a very joyful pillow, she is never without a smile!

One day, she got invited to Unicorn's party, but unfortunately she was also invited to McDonald's on the exact same time and day. Happyia sat in her bed worrying about where she should go.

"What am I to do?" she cried. Suddenly, there was a loud *swoop!* It was Owly!

"I've been listening to your words. I'll give you five words. Look on the bright side!"

It worked! Happyia had a lovely time at Unicorn's party! She could go to McDonald's any time she likes.

Mawadda Babiker Elnur (8)

Furzefield Primary School, Merstham

Adventure In Storytopia

Sarah had about one hundred toys from different famous stories, and she enjoyed playing with them. One night, she dreamt her toys came to life and that she joined them to travel to a place called Storytopia. While there, she changed to the main characters in the stories which included Belle, Ariel, Cinderella, Snow White, etc. She had lots of fun becoming the princess in each story.

When morning came, she woke up and found all her story figures had changed to toys. She was, however, very happy because she knew she'd just had an experience of a lifetime.

Mildred Iziegbe Omoruyi (9)
Furzefield Primary School, Merstham

Jack And Robodog

On Christmas Day, Jack got a Robodog from
Santa. Jack took Robodog out for the family walk
down by the wide and deep river near the house.
Everyone was really excited to go on a rowing boat
down the river. Suddenly, Jack fell backwards into
the stormy water. Robodog tried to rescue him
before it was too late. Robodog cautiously
dragged him back into the boat. He saved Jack,
but Jack was extremely sad because Robodog got
wet and went fizzle and stopped working. But
because Jack loved him so much, that night Santa
turned Robodog into a real dog.

Robert Potter (8)
Furzefield Primary School, Merstham

The Game Of Chess!

Once, there was a chessboard and on it were some chess pieces. Suddenly, the white and the black kings declared war! The pieces lined up, ready for attack. White moved first and the black struck. Soon all the pawns were gone... then the rooks and the knights. Some time later, all of the bishops vanished, black and white. Blacks' next move made white angry because the black queen took out the white queen. White avenged the queen by taking out the black queen. Now, just the white and the black kings were left... so they decided to be friends!

Harrison Gurney (8)
Furzefield Primary School, Merstham

Barbie Finds A Friend

Once upon a time, there was a beautiful Barbie. She lived in an enormous mansion. She had lots of money which made her rich. The only thing she didn't have was friends. That made Barbie feel so lonely. She really wanted to find friends.
So one day she decided to go to the park. When she was there, she met a girl and was chatting. As they told each other about themselves they became really close friends. Then she decided to book a ticket for a ball and she met lots more. They lived happily ever after.

Zoe Pinto (8)
Furzefield Primary School, Merstham

Dragster Racing

Whoosh! Sammy drove like the wind when he was on his last lap. But Paul and Holly were starting to close in on him. As they got closer to the finish line, Amy sped off leaving them in a cloud of dust. Ten seconds later, when he was about 80 metres from the racing cup, Holly and Paul caught up again and *poof!* It was a photo-finish. Sammy pulled in and nervously looked at the screen. Fortunately, it said that he had come first! His teammates Abigail, Kate and Joe happily congratulated him and later fixed his toy boosters.

Seth Dayo-Somefun (8)

Furzefield Primary School, Merstham

The Missing Teddy Bear

Once upon a time, there was a little girl who wanted a teddy bear for Christmas.

One day on Christmas Eve, a girl called Amy wrote on her Christmas list she only wanted a teddy bear for Christmas. She went to bed for a couple of hours. Then all of a sudden it was morning. Amy woke up in a hurry, she wanted to see her present underneath her Christmas tree. She ran to her wrapping and opened the box, she saw a teddy. She kissed the teddy and she loved him forever and ever. They lived happily ever after.

Zaneta Ndhlovu (8)

Furzefield Primary School, Merstham

The Brave Armodrillo

Under my duvet, a toy is wandering. He gets out the duvet.

"Wow it's so dark, woah, I'm melting," Armodrillo whispers, he has fallen off the bed and is now on the floor.

He tries everything but it never works. Then he gets an idea, he climbs onto the toy box and grabs Four Arms. Then they both jump and make it to the bed and he stops melting. Also he never ever will go out or over the cover again, and always plays with Overflow forever and ever. But Four Arms gets off the big bed again...

Dominic John Blore (8)

Furzefield Primary School, Merstham

A Wrestle-Off

One day, George was playing with his wrestlers when his mum shouted up, "It's time for school." So George rushed downstairs.
While he was gone all the wrestlers did nothing until the wrestlers sat up. They were alive! They ate George's advent calendar, they messed up his room, broke everything until they challenged each other to a wrestle. John Cena lost, he was so angry he thought he was the strongest. "Rrrr!"
Then George came home and John Cena realised it was just a dream.

George Higgs (9)
Furzefield Primary School, Merstham

Demi The Doll

Once, there was a doll called Demi. She was stuck in a box. She was fighting and budging to get out. Finally, she broke out the box. She wanted to get out the toy store. So she sneaked about but the manager was right next to the door, so she wandered around the store. She saw loads of toys still in their boxes. The manager went and Demi didn't know he'd gone. So Demi went back to the doll aisle and saw that he'd gone. So she went to the door and went out and she lived happily ever after.

Brooke Shelley (8)
Furzefield Primary School, Merstham

Magic Football

While playing in my garden, I heard *bang, bang!* I ran over to the shed where the noise was coming from. I opened the shed door and the football bounced into the garden. The football seemed to have a mind of its own. When I tried to kick it, the ball moved away from me before my foot kicked it. It happened again and again. I went upstairs and changed into my Crystal Palace football kit. As if by magic, I was scoring goals and playing amazing football that I had never played before in my life.

James Booker (8)

Furzefield Primary School, Merstham

Big Bunny's Adventure

Big Bunny slipped off the bed. Sioned rolled over. Big Bunny rubbed his eyes and looked around, he had never been in a tent before. He unzipped the door. Big Bunny hopped out onto the grass. He wanted to see the chickens Sioned had told him about. He hopped up the hill. There was a sign on the fence, it was a warning telling you the fence was electrified. He suddenly missed Sioned, and the warm sleeping bag. He hopped back into the tent. He climbed into Sioned's bed. She put her arm around him.

Sioned Marshall-Jones (8)
Furzefield Primary School, Merstham

Dalmation, The Adopted Puppy Teddy

Hello, my name is Dalmation. I was born in Ikea. It was really big, scary and lonely there.

One day, I was adopted by Matt for a little blue-eyed girl called Chloe who was two years old. Chloe cuddled me closely. She kissed me and even nibbled my ear like my mummy used to. I'm a little worn out but I'm seven. You know it's not easy living with a nine-year-old if you know what I mean, but she does love me, so so much. I could not have a better owner. We are best friends forever, always.

Chloe Lewis (9)

Furzefield Primary School, Merstham

The Amazing Race

Once there was a toy motorbike. One day, he decided to join the 2018 World Motorbike Championship. He got a place and was so happy, his number was 11.

A few months later it was race day. In a few hours the race began. First, he was in third place, suddenly he spotted a short cut which was Rainbow Road from Mario Kart 8, he was so excited. He was on his fifth lap out of 25, he started on Rainbow Road, he nearly fell off but didn't, it was so close. They had a battle, but he finished second.

Ryan O'Neill (8)
Furzefield Primary School, Merstham

Home Sweet Home

On a grey, gloomy battlefield, a teddy was lying. It was the end of the war, he had twisted his paw. There was a sound in the distance, a woof. Timmy the teddy lay there still as a statue. The barking came nearer, a small poodle! The poodle came nearer. Timmy realised it was Dylan (his young mistress' dog).

"How great it is to see you again," piped up Timmy.

"Come along then," barked Dylan.

So Timmy went home with Dylan the dog.

Eleanor Bass (9)

Furzefield Primary School, Merstham

The Lost Bear

One morning, Fluffy the bear jumped out of the little girl's bedroom window and onto the road. Fluffy ran quickly down the long road to the South Ferry Port. He climbed on a random boat and wondered where he'd go to. There he met a crowd of schoolgirls who wanted the irresistible bear and took it!

The schoolgirls left the bear on a rock and forgot about it. Fluffy was really, really lonely and sad, but then saw Nessie with a pink cute bear! There, their journey continues.

Scarlett Tse (8)

Furzefield Primary School, Merstham

The Doll Who Wanted A Sister

Once upon a time, there lived a doll who wanted a sister. One day, she decided to leave a note for her owner, and her owner Daisy read it.

So a few days later, they went to the toyshop and they were sold out! So they tried again and again, but they were sold out. Now they had to just wait and wait.

A few days later, they had a break from getting a sister but, when they went again, they were there. Rose (my doll) was really happy so they got one and Rose had a sister.

Daisy Walton (8)

Furzefield Primary School, Merstham

Angel's Life Of An Alien

Once, there lived a toy alien called Angel, but she had lost her parents, so she lived alone. She was only three years old when her parents went away.
After thirty years, she met another alien called Stitch who also lost his parents, and they wanted to get married. It took years and years to plan and after five years they got married.
Then they heard me coming into the room and I shouted, "What is going on here?"

Georgia Gladman (8)
Furzefield Primary School, Merstham

The Dog Who Didn't Have A Home

Once upon a time, there lived a toy dog who had no home, he found a road and crossed it. He slowly walked to a house, he tried to get them to open the door but they wouldn't. Finally they opened the door, so they took him into their house. They kept him for such a long time, but one day a new baby was born, so they didn't give him as much attention, but he was still happy.

Macie Jane Macpherson (8)
Furzefield Primary School, Merstham

Savage Attack

"I want new toys!" demanded Cindy.

"What's wrong with the ones you already have?" asked Linda, Cindy's mum.

"Look at it, it's headless!"

Linda shrugged her shoulders but said nothing.

Cindy narrowed her pupils and aimed them at her mum's dark, sapphire eyes.

That night, Daffles the unicorn held a meeting.

"We must teach Cindy a lesson," Daffles stated.

Daffles pounced onto Cindy and screamed, "Attack!" Nonchalantly, Daffles flew onto Cindy and asked, "Will you ever chuck us around again?"

"No, no! I won't!" promised Cindy.

Now Cindy's learnt her lesson never to disrespect her toys ever again.

Olivia Kraus (9)
Guildford High School, Guildford

The Boxing Champion

It was a noisy day in the bedroom. A pink horse was telling his penguin friend he was entering the boxing championships.

"I'm not sure," said the penguin as he turned away.

"I'm entering the boxing championships for tomorrow," the horse mumbled to himself... After a while, he went to sleep.

The next day, "I'm at the championships," smiled the horse. "What's that noise?" asked the horse to his opponent.

Unexpectedly, someone yelled, "The human!"

We all lay still.

"What's going on?" exclaimed the boy. "Whatever, I'm going back to sleep,' said the boy.

So the horse won the championships.

Claudia Timmerman (9)
Guildford High School, Guildford

The Melon-Eating Monster

Tom stomped down for breakfast while Sergeant Stuffy and Sergeant Sting were talking.

"Let's find the melon-eating monster!" exclaimed Sergeant Sting.

"Okay," followed Sergeant Stuffy.

In just a few hours, it became bedtime for Tom but adventure time for them. So they quietly slid downstairs and hid behind the fridge. They heard a noise and jumped out, the melon monster was there!

"Stranger danger," replied Sting.

"Is there an echo in here?"

"No!" answered the melon monster.

"Oh," Stuffy replied.

"Uhh!" Sting exclaimed, hitting his head really hard!

The following morning Tom got his melon and he was happy!

Lucy Turner (8)
Guildford High School, Guildford

Christmas Catastrophe

"Psst!" came a low hiss. "The Its have gone!"
At midnight sharp, in the dead of the night, Coco, a
crystal cat ornament, crept out with all the Barbie
dolls and together they planned to damage
objects and destroy everything each Christmas.
This year, they decided to steal all the sweets and
presents in the stockings.
"Let's climb up the Christmas tree,
Sherlock Holmes style!"
Valentina the Barbie drove them over and they
climbed silently up the Christmas tree. Suddenly,
footsteps... Adele's mum came stalking in viciously.
She didn't see Coco and headed in the opposite
direction. They were safe!

Adele Kenenbayeva (9)
Guildford High School, Guildford

The Adventure Of Brambles And Pinkie

"Dinner!" Melissa barked. Melissa was Hanna's foster mother and she was revolting. Hanna stomped down the stairs and into the grey kitchen. I stood up. My name is Brambles. I am a toy deer.

"Pinkie!" I muttered.

Out of the cupboard trotted a large piggy bank.

"Right! Let's get back to our mission to climb the bedside table!"

So we snatched our ropes and started scaling the table. Eventually, we reached the top.

"We did it! We... Ahh!" Pinkie screamed as her leg shattered.

Suddenly, I heard a creak.

"I'll fix her," sighed Hanna. That's how Hanna knows we can talk.

Isobel Browne (8)
Guildford High School, Guildford

Puddles - Moving House

"Puddles, look!" exclaimed Darcy Greenfold. It was Darcy's last day to play with Puddles, her favourite toy bear, until tomorrow when they moved house. *Hmm*, thought Darcy, *I'll leave Puddles*.

The next day, they set off in the morning. It took thirty minutes to get there. The new house was sensational. Meanwhile, Puddles had managed to climb out of the bin and followed them.

"Hmm..." wondered Darcy. She was wondering why Puddles was here. "Oh well!" said Darcy. She put Puddles on the bedside table.

Now Puddles the teddy bear is loved very much by Darcy and Lily Greenfold.

Hanna Naqvi (9)
Guildford High School, Guildford

Here Comes Trouble...

"Psst, the... the... Things have gone," whispered Berry Cream cheekily.

"Time to take action!" Berry Churro replied deviously.

To the gargantuan Things' room they went as if they were the characters of Mission Impossible. The 'up to no good' duo started to invade the cupboards.

"Ooh how about this one?"

"Or this one?" Berry Churro was actually about to rip up Mum's best dress! "Now Mum's favourite dress has gone!"

"Down to the triple fudge trifle..."

The fridge in the kitchen held this mouth-watering treat.

Just then the lock clicked.

Zara Ahmad (9)
Guildford High School, Guildford

Graffiti Artist

Dark, gloomy... An alleyway was a perfect setting for this story. *Ssss!* The townspeople fled inside as a creature stepped out, it was... a graffiti artist... toy unicorn hit the alleyway. *Ssss!* Spray cans released their paint. The villain stopped and admired its work.

"You cops come get me!" she rapped. "I'm the most wanted villain in the world!" She stared into the darkness. "My work here is done!"

She slung the spray cans over her shoulder! She returned and wrote 'Rebecca is the rebel!' But as she turned around, she was in trouble, cop cars were surrounding her! Oops!

Molly Hope (8)
Guildford High School, Guildford

The Island Fight

It was a dreary morning as John left his room. As soon as John left, the toy tribe (led by Jaz) and the Lego tribe (led by Alandra) had an argument.

They both wanted to own the island in the middle of John's room. The battle was violent, there were swords slashing and arrows firing.

Suddenly the door creaked open.

"Freeze!" shouted Jaz.

"He's back,' screamed Alandra.

All the Lego and toy soldiers scrambled back to their positions. Whilst frozen, everyone discovered how silly they were and the next day decided to rule the island together in peace and harmony.

Audrey Yendole (8)
Guildford High School, Guildford

The Rich Bear

On Monday, Disco the bear awoke. Cheekily, she grabbed her dress and shoes and got into her golden Rolls Royce in order to drive to her friend's house to pick up Dior.

"Hey, let's go to the train station and get a ride to Olivia's school," she smirked. When Disco and Dior arrived, the headmaster was still there, so they sneaked in through the chimney. As Dior hit the ground, the headmaster screamed, "Who's there?" They were caught! The headmaster called Olivia to come and get them and then he insisted that she put them both in the garbage.

Evita Troman (8)
Guildford High School, Guildford

Pig Troubles

In a pink palace lived a pink toy pig called Mr Piggy. Without a sound, he was sleeping in his brown bed when suddenly he was dreaming that a mud monster was coming through an air vent. Mr Piggy woke up in shock. "Ahh!" he screamed. "Who are you?"

"I am a mud monster," replied the monster.

"What? A mud monster? Ahh!"

"Yes!"

Was it happening now at this very moment at this very time? He had no choice. He was confused for the very first time. It was getting creepier and creepier. It was real.

Scarlett Cooper (8)
Guildford High School, Guildford

Untitled

In a very untidy bedroom, stood three toys on one bed. One was a very sneaky rabbit toy called Hoppy. One bear toy was really naughty as well and he was called Harry. And the last one was extremely silly, he was a toy dog called Freddie. Their owner was called Tony.

Once the toys' family left for the weekend, they started to tease the house. Hoppy knocked all of the books down from the bookshelf. Harry put the plug in for the sink and turned the taps on. Freddie locked the front door.

"Oh no," cried Harry. "They're coming!"

Fleur Hall (8)
Guildford High School, Guildford

The Kitchen Mess-Up By Sophia And Tom!

As soon as Princess Mia was asleep, Sophia the bunny who had jet-black eyes and elephant-grey fur, crept down into the kitchen and opened the cupboard where all of the food was kept. However, before Sophia could even reach out for the food, she heard a deep rumbling voice behind her... as soon as Sophia turned around, she saw Tom. Tom, who had a big thunderous voice and hazelnut-brown fur was smiling at her.

"Hello Sophia, out for a little wander in the kitchen eh?"

"Tom never mind what I'm doing, let's mess up the kitchen!"

"Yeah!"

Keira Olivia Oxley (8)
Guildford High School, Guildford

Ginger And The Bakery

One day, Ginger the toy cat was taking a stroll down the brick wall of his neighbour's garden. Ginger was an unusual cat because he was a ginger Siamese, with ebony eyes. His neighbour, Tom, was a grey tomcat with emerald eyes. Ginger took no notice of him as he strutted by. His favourite place in the whole of Mouser Lake was the bakery. He entered from the back door. The front of the shop was owned by a malt-coloured tabby. The back of the shop was rented by Ginger's business, 'Siamese'. He turned the handle. *Squeak, squeak, squeak!*

Chloe Abbott (9)
Guildford High School, Guildford

Mr Fatty And Me

When I woke up Mr Fatty, my teddy pig, was gone! "Finally I have escaped," exclaimed Mr Fatty. "I'm free!"

I was so devastated he was gone! I was crying my head off so I told Mum and she said, "He'll turn up I'm sure." She put her arm around me.

One month later, still no sign of him.

Tomorrow he'll show up I'm sure. And I was right. He was there on my bed. I hugged him so hard even Mum came up and I whispered, "I love you so much Mr Fatty. I love you so, so much!"

Lauren Ellis (8)
Guildford High School, Guildford

The Chess Tournament

Jaya had two toys: a lion called Blade and a pony called Jasper (a strawberry Roan). In the morning, everyone woke up. Blade tiptoed into a tent and lay there. Suddenly, a shadow loomed over the whole room. Luckily, it was only Jaya. Soon after, Jaya had slammed the door and was off to her chess tournament. The toys leapt out of their hiding space and started looking for the chessboard.

"No, Jaya has taken the chessboard with her. Let's make a paper chessboard."

The chessboard had all sorts of materials and they had the time of their life.

Jaya Mangat (8)
Guildford High School, Guildford

Golden Duck

There are nine ducks, each one a different colour; the leader's golden, deputy leader is silver, then the servants. The first is red, the second is orange, the third is yellow, the fourth is green, the fifth is blue, the sixth is purple, the seventh is pink. One day, Bob was awake in his comfortable bed. The toys were lying on the bedroom floor stock-still. After a while, Bob fell asleep and the ducks awoke and waddled into their positions ready to play with poop and fire it at humans, but it did not work because the poop was dry.

Annabella Higgins (8)
Guildford High School, Guildford

The Problems Of The Toys

One bright and sunny morning, Fudge, Ted, Purdy and Cheshy woke up and yawned. Fudge was a dog. Ted was a teddy. Purdy was a moshi-monster. Cheshy was a cat. They crept down the stairs and entered the kitchen. They made their way to the playroom but they had to pass the hamster's room. The hamster's name was Biscuit and they had woken her up... Biscuit scrambled out of her cage using claws and chased them. Then the EV3 turned on and grabbed them. The Lego dragon flew up and hastily rescued them and carried them back to bed.

Jemma Kuhnert (9)
Guildford High School, Guildford

The Mischievous Toys

Once upon a time, there was a bunny called Miffy. There was also a toy called Picacho. Miffy and Picacho were very mischievous! When I came back from school, they were never where I left them. Once, they were sitting on the fan and Dad had to get them down! I wonder what they are going to do today?

Whilst I was at school, I found that they had ripped up my homework and they had chucked my duvet out of the window, and they had a very big disco. As you can see they are very, very mischievous!

Annabel Goodworth (8)
Guildford High School, Guildford

Dog Diving

One day, there were two toys called Stitch and QES (Queen Elizabeth Stieff). Stitch was sky-blue with dark blue stripes. They realised QES had lost her crown, so they looked on the security camera to find out that the Singleton's family dog, Jack, had eaten the crown! Stitch went to get some diving gear and as quick as a flash they were inside the tummy of Jack! They swam for what seemed like hours. Passing some of Mr Singleton's glasses that he, Jack, had eaten a month ago, they found her crown. QES was happy.

Arabella Singleton (8)
Guildford High School, Guildford

Cuddles On The Roll

My owner rolled off her bed, grabbed her bag and raced down the stairs, while I sneakily somersaulted off the top bunk of her miraculously tall bunk bed. I started by making the bed a tip, but I'm sorry I was only looking for Melanie Unicorn, and on the bright side, I found her. I whispered to her some random words that she seemed to understand. We ran down the stairs with excitement. In front of us, Melanie spotted a vacuum cleaner. I tripped and fell headfirst on the carpet. I couldn't walk, I'd broken my foot...

Louise O'Hara (8)
Guildford High School, Guildford

The Forgotten Toys

In a sky-blue cottage lived a girl, Millie, who played with us toys. Before long, Millie grew up and chucked us in the attic. After a while, we decided to escape. We tried so hard that Puddles broke! As if by magic, a brand-new toy appeared! The toy had moveable arms so we finally escaped the box. Downstairs, we could hear Millie's aunt chatting away. As fast as we could, we ran to the box and jumped back in. The aunt took us, she did! But instead of keeping us she sold us to the boring charity shop!

Maia Greaves (8)
Guildford High School, Guildford

I Know

When the family leave the house, nobody knows what Dreamer and Sunshine do. Only I know!
I pretended to close the door so they thought we were gone but I was hiding under the bed, watching every move they made. Today Mum, Dad and Thea went shopping and I hid under the bed. Where do you think they went? First, they went to the kitchen and ate half the biscuit tin. But then they ran upstairs to my room.
My family came through the door and were so cross with me, it was unbelievable.

Phoebe Forrest-Biggs (8)
Guildford High School, Guildford

Mission To Sweetie-Filled Stocking

Suddenly, the sitting room door slammed shut. The Fixit twins, Mike and Kate, slipped their spanners back into their belts. The new toy convertible was built. Time for Plan A. Tommy got into his green car seat and everyone else got in too with the pets. As the engine roared, they zoomed faster, making a beeline for the sweets in Orla's stocking. But they spun out of control and Mike slammed on the brakes and they flew into the stocking and ate all the sweets.
What will Orla say?

J Paton (8)
Guildford High School, Guildford

The Teddy Bears' Picnic

"Ugh picnics are really, really boring!" declared Brown Ted dully.

"If you are going to be grumpy you can stay at home," replied Mother Bear.

Her hands were full as she was holding two baskets of sandwiches, cakes and lemonade. Walking behind her was Baby Ted who could not wait to have the picnic. After what felt like forever, they arrived at the meadow. Yum!

Everything tasted so good. Brown Ted especially liked the jam sandwiches.

"I love pink icing," exclaimed Baby Ted. "I can't wait to eat more."

"I can't wait to get you to bed," laughed Mother Bear.

Unaiza Bachlani (9)

Kew Riverside Primary School, Richmond

The Extraordinary Dream!

As I stood up, I walked towards a weird shadow behind the enormous tree. I went closer till... goodness! It was a toy monster. I couldn't tell the gender but it was a green, furry, and scary-looking creature. I stealthily tiptoed behind the wall. It looked at me and growled. "Excuse me... hello," I said, walking closer. After that we had a picnic. We became best friends. At last it spoke to me...
"Wake up darling, it's already eight o'clock."
I sat up. It turned out to be a dream, but I'll never forget that green, furry and friendly monster.

Sona Khamar (10)
Kew Riverside Primary School, Richmond

Alive!

Flusssshhhh. That's all I heard. With a start, I wondered what and where the sound was coming from. I followed the sound and shock took over my body. My toy room had come alive! My dolls were wandering around, some were dancing and singing. I took a step closer. It was the doll's house toilet that was flushing. I was speechless.
"Hello," one of the dolls said and invited me in. There were tea and cakes too. The dolls all had beautiful bright eyes and slender feet with red patent shoes.
That's when I heard my alarm clock *trinnnggg!*

Sana Hanief (9)
Kew Riverside Primary School, Richmond

Toy Story

"Boss, I see the enemy!" whispered Soldier One.

"Great!" said the boss. "Now we need to creep out of this place."

"You're right," said Soldier Three, horrified.

"Boss, we're creeping out, meet us at the factory okay?"

"Okay," said the boss. "I'm just trying to get past the enemies."

"We're coming to help," said all the soldiers.

"Then come and help," said the boss.

"We're coming!" shouted the soldiers.

The soldiers won their fight and they lived very well.

"That was very hard," said Soldier One feeling excited.

"Yes it was," said Soldier Three.

Harry Liston (8)
Marden Lodge Primary School, Caterham

Mischief In Toys 'R' Us

"Barbie," said Disco Man, "the coast is clear."

"Yah," said Barbie, "it's time to have a disco party."

"Oh yeah, you're right," said Disco Man. "Come on it's time for a party."

Then they danced the night away. As they danced and danced they ate some cake and knocked some of the toys. How naughty is that?

Then suddenly the unicorn appeared, "What's going on?"

"Well," said Barbie, smiling at Disco Man. "It's a long story..."

"Quick, the manager is coming. It's morning! People are going to buy us," said Disco Man!

"We've spent too much time dancing, oh no!"

Amela Selimaj (7)
Marden Lodge Primary School, Caterham

No Escape, Toys!

"Tie them up!" Ted commanded. He was the General of Toymania.

"Please don't!" Barbie and Ken exclaimed in unison.

"I won't get my beauty sleep ever again!" complained Barbie.

"I'll lose all my clothes!" muttered Ken.

Barbie nudged him on the shoulder.

Ted was now furious! He was turning redder by the second.

"Stormtrooper robots, assemble. Make sure the crocodiles bite their tiny toes!"

"Crocodiles?" Ken screamed worriedly.

"Yes, you deserve torture because you tried to escape. You were also blabbering!" Ted was crazy!

"Take them away!" He ordered...

Alex Frith (9)
Marden Lodge Primary School, Caterham

Secret Party

Ballerina pirouetted off her music box. "We could plan a party for Alfie's seventh birthday."
The toys had been arguing about his birthday for hours. But they disagreed, until one hour later it was decided on the party. Alfie was at school, it was 1:30pm.
"Right soldiers, you're in charge of the balloons! Barbie dolls, the birthday cake!" commanded the King.
"What are you going to do then?" asked Harry Kane rudely.
"Relax, anyway what does it have to do with you!" boomed the King.
"Okay, okay let's forget all of this, the 100-layered cake is ready!" butted in Barbie...

Katie Morrison (8)
Marden Lodge Primary School, Caterham

Soldier And The Lamborghini

"Sergeant, coast is clear, I'm scanning."

"Progress?"

"No enemies found yet Sergeant."

But one minute later, enemies came for attack.

"Lambo drive me over and get fighting with me."

So they fought until they heard a noise, they all hid under the bed but all it was was the mum and dad checking. As soon as they closed the door, Sergeant shouted, "Attack!" Then they attacked, then soon the fight ended.

"Help," shouted Sergeant, stuck. So Lambo drove and pulled Sergeant out, but as soon as he got pulled out they saw the child wake up, they scattered away.

Crystal Collins (8)

Marden Lodge Primary School, Caterham

Toy Story

"Ahh! I'm getting broken up into little pieces!" shouted Harry. "Ooh! I'm suddenly in a mech robot, now I can help all the toys to escape from the bedroom. Yes I can finally escape the bedroom."
It was their only chance to escape. Every day they would find them in a different shape or size.
"Formation!"
"Sergeant Booboo!"
"Yes, yes it's me now we have an attack in a couple of minutes."
"How do you know?"
"Because I checked the dinner table and I saw them eating spaghetti! Well at least." *Creak.* "Run for your life...!"

Harry Cotterrill (9)
Marden Lodge Primary School, Caterham

Rainbow The Lost Unicorn

One beautiful day, Sarah went to Disneyland Paris. She got ready and took her teddy Rainbow with her. Sarah was playing on such marvellous games and rides that she forgot all about Rainbow! Sarah finally realised that she had lost Rainbow the unicorn. She was so sad and felt full of guilt.
Then she was asking everyone but no one helped her.
Someone whispered, "It's going to take a very long time to find her in this place!"
All of a sudden, Sarah saw Rainbow with a child and got her back.
"I'm sorry Rainbow," said Sarah. "Hooray!"

Kristal Harrocks (10)
Marden Lodge Primary School, Caterham

The Pirate Who Found The Treasure

"Arr!" said a pirate on a ship with his crew.
"Captain, we need to go south," said Ben the pirate.
So they went.
"Aarr, what?" said the second pirate.
"There's a black hole made out of water. Arr!"
They went spinning like a cheetah running in circles. They spun and spun and then there was no water left.
"What happened?" said the pirate.
"OMG! I found the treasure!"
"Hello," said the captain, but then he saw a pirate, he thought it was a fish, but it was a pirate. They got out of the bath and met a large man.

Aidan Bassant (7)
Marden Lodge Primary School, Caterham

Unicorn Toys Into Human Size

One summer morning, Daisy woke up and as she got up she knocked her water bottle on the floor. It fell on her unicorn toys as she walked out her room for breakfast. The unicorns started growing! The biggest unicorn was bright pink. Suddenly, she began to speak, "My name is Rainbow."

Then a green one said quietly, "Nice to meet you, my name's Fluffy."

Daisy came back in and she got such a fright, but Rainbow said, "Don't be scared, we're just friendly unicorns!"

So Daisy and her two unicorns became friends and then she became a terrific unicorn.

Lily Carter (9)

Marden Lodge Primary School, Caterham

The Horrifying World Of FNAF!

One deadly, deserted night, a bunch of deserting figures came to life one night. They were the worst toys ever, they took down buildings.

"Ha ha," said one of the toys, her name was Bonnie.

Bonnie wasn't alone she was with a group. There was one toy that was called Freddy. Freddy was Captain, the rest were called Magel, Foxy and others. They were deadly until they met their doom... It was the great Kraken, the biggest sea beast ever. The FNAF gang tried until they defeated her. They were heroes, people loved them and they changed forever and ever.

Patrick Draper (9)
Marden Lodge Primary School, Caterham

Escape Mum

"The coast is clear, Sir! But hurry, he could wake up any time!" whispered Jack, the jack-in-the-box.

"Yay, but wait... how are we going to get the lid off?" shouted the leader.

"I know," whispered a little boy called Max.

"Thank you Max. We're trying to get away from the monster under your bed. You put us in the wrong box too."

"Oh that monster under my bed is my cat, now hurry, get in my hands quickly!" As the toys jumped into Max's hands he heard his mum coming up the stairs. She was very close!

Evie Hunt (9)

Marden Lodge Primary School, Caterham

The Girl Lost The Dolls

The girl is playing with her dolls called
Sasey Summer and Sasey Stephen, then she goes
to the toilet. Her mum sees her toys on the floor so
she picks them up because they might break if Dad
steps on them.

"I should pick them up."

When the girl is finished in the toilet, she goes in
her room, she looks around, she says, "Where's
my toys? Mum come here now!"

"Yes, what's the matter?"

"Do you know where my toys are?"

"Yes, they are in your toy box."

"Thank you Mum."

Summer Rose (8)
Marden Lodge Primary School, Caterham

The Teddy's Sleepover

There is a teddy called Freddy.
One night, they are sleeping under Lucas' bed and
see a monster called Paige. Paige is Lucas' little
sister. She gets angry really easily. That's why
people call her a monster. Ciara and Freddy
need all the help they can get from Lucas. Lucas is
their only friend. The teddies, Ciara and Freddy,
always hang out with Lucas, they think he's really
cool. Paige the monster ends up looking different
and really pretty, then likes sleeping in Lucas' bed.
She's really cute now.

Talia Rose Cole (8)
Marden Lodge Primary School, Caterham

Bebe And Santa

One day, Bebe went to Toys 'R' Us and saw an arrestment kit, but that was £50. But at least she had £50. Then she was shocked, she saw a kid's motorbike that she could actually ride, but that was £100, so she went home. She got £100 but as soon as she got to Toys 'R' Us, there was no more left.

She woke up on Christmas Day and had some cupcakes for breakfast and opened her presents. She saw everything she wanted, so she wrote to Santa and said, 'Thank you for everything. I'm going to play outside'.

Chanaé McLean (7)
Marden Lodge Primary School, Caterham

Pluto The Lost Dog

One exciting morning, Aaliyah and her family went to Disneyland, a place of adventures. They went on lots of different rides such as Hyper Space Mountain, shooting games and many more. After that they went to a shop with lots of squishy, furry teddies and there was one that caught Aaliyah's eye, it was a colossal yellow-eyed dog, and she just had to buy it, so she did.

Since then she's never left its side until one Tuesday afternoon, disaster struck, they were on their way to their next destination and the yellow-eyed dog was never found.

Aaliyah Wright (9)

Marden Lodge Primary School, Caterham

Jake L's Toy Lightsaber Story!

"Captain?" said the green lightsaber.

"Yes," said the brown lightsaber.

Then the red lightsaber slashed the brown one.

"Well I just sadly killed you!" he exclaimed.

Then he slashed all the controls and the ship went down.

"Mayday, Mayday going down, going down!" said the pilot, and the ship went down.

All the sabers died apart from the green and red. They had a fight. The green won but then Kylo's saber had a fight and the green won again, and he fixed the ship and then flew away.

Jake Learner (8)
Marden Lodge Primary School, Caterham

The Talking Teddy Bear

"What is this place?" said Tilly to herself. She had just been put in a doll's house. Tilly spent a good five minutes trying to find out what this place was until a human had come in to play with Tilly.
Tilly screamed while the human was creeping up to her, so the human said very loud. "You can talk!"
After that they were talking to each other and then Tilly said, "My name is Tilly, do you want to be my friend?"
And he said, "Yes my name is Freddie," and they both lived happily ever after.

Molly Flood (9)
Marden Lodge Primary School, Caterham

The Gorilla And The Car

The gorilla tries to break the car, the car's too fast for the gorilla. He's becoming very angry and stomping his feet viciously. The car revs his engine viciously. Gorilla is punching his chest, he sees the car is getting away and goes under the bed. Gorilla breaks the bed to get to him, he just wants to be his friend, but the car is scared of him. Then the toys get put away. They manage to leap through the door, the car agrees to be friends with Gorilla. Gorilla picks the car up and spins around, the car screams.

Leah Holly Hills (8)
Marden Lodge Primary School, Caterham

The New Favourite Toy

I was bought in the shop by a little boy and he took me home and played with me. I was his new favourite toy, but just then the boy called Paige got a new toy and he called it Tom. Paige played with us both. All of a sudden, Paige's room was turned into a Tom overload. His bedsheets changed, his wallpaper, his pictures and photos around his mirror.

"What happened?" I said. "OMG!"

I was no longer his favourite toy anymore. Tom took over the bedroom. All of the other toys couldn't believe their eyes, Tom couldn't either.

Tamzin O'Leary (8)

Marden Lodge Primary School, Caterham

Lost Unicorn

One day, there was a girl called Grace and she had a toy unicorn called Rainbow. It was Grace's favourite toy. But one day, Grace was having breakfast and she had left Rainbow upstairs and when Grace went upstairs, Rainbow was gone. Grace said to her mum, "Rainbow isn't upstairs." Her mum said, "Well let's go look."

They had looked everywhere but then they saw her outside going onto a boat, so they went outside to look and Rainbow was on a boat. So Grace took Rainbow back to her bedroom, and locked her in the bedroom.

Kaia Chapman (9)
Marden Lodge Primary School, Caterham

The Unicorn And The Girl

Once, there was a toy called Sparkle. She never got seen or bought.

One day, there was a girl called Lucy, she loved unicorns. Sparkle got really excited. She tried to move, but luckily she didn't. The girl got Sparkle. When they were walking around the shop she saw a big bag, so she got it and put Sparkle in the bag. When she got home she went to get Sparkle but she wasn't there! Thankfully, she was found. Lucy put Sparkle somewhere safe, so she was not going to get lost ever again, they were very happy together.

Jamiella Farina (7)

Marden Lodge Primary School, Caterham

Robotic Turned Bad

Two bots were playing in their garden. They were playing catch. Robotic threw the ball, it fell backwards. His brother told him to go and retrieve it. When he did, his brother found a friend. He was very mad. He was so mad he turned evil. He turned into Robotic Snapper. Then all of a sudden he tried to snap Flamer, his brother, to twelve pieces, but he missed. Next he was aiming for his friend. He snipped and snapped. He was so mad he was going to shoot his laser. He shot his laser. His brother stopped him.

Samuel Bradley (7)
Marden Lodge Primary School, Caterham

The Soldier And The Lamborghini

The soldier and the Lambo are getting ready for the race.

"Ready, steady, go!" and off they go.

They go around the corner, hit a jump and they're nearly at the finish line. They go around another corner and as they go around the corner,
they crash! They keep going, the other cars overtake them.They are now in last place, they are very sad.

But wait, they're putting their boosters on, they finally overtake them, they are so happy.

They are so close to the finish and, yes, they win!

Stephen Lyons (8)

Marden Lodge Primary School, Caterham

Mr Candy's Toy Troubles

Once upon a time, I woke up as a toy. I was my candy toy!

"Woah! I'm a toy!"

I was amazed but scared since I didn't know how to go back to normal. First, I tried to shoot candy at myself but nothing happened. Next, I tried eating my candy-self but that just broke my tooth. Then I went to the swimming pool to drown myself, but still nothing.

I was just about to lose hope when I was struck by a brilliant idea! *Jump off the desk!* I took a big run-up and I went *splat!*

Nicolas Mills (10)

Marden Lodge Primary School, Caterham

My Llama Story

My name is Normey, the one-horned toy llama. I live in the worst place ever, it's called Dump Land. I wish I could go to a fun and exciting place. I think I live with a man called Farmer Joe. I really just want to explore the world, actually I could now. Farmer Joe is gone so we could!

Five minutes later, why did we choose to go? I do see a colourful land, let's go...

One minute later, sorry about the wait I'm just having too much fun with my friend Boogey Boy. Sorry I have to go now.

Daisy Martin (9)
Marden Lodge Primary School, Caterham

The Toy Vs The Evil Toy

One dark, gloomy day, it was me that just woke up in Toys 'R' Us. Everyone hated me and didn't care about me, but suddenly my dream came true! A boy that was petrified picked me up, then he smiled as soon as he picked me up. After he bought me he called me Mr Pokémon.

The boy thought, *if I dropped Mr Pokémon will he walk or not?* So as soon as he dropped me the evil Hoopa appeared, so I had to fight him. I used my special move, super clone punch, and I knocked him over!

Jedi Amponsah (10)

Marden Lodge Primary School, Caterham

Kong Goes To Town

Once upon a time, there was a toy Kong, he wanted to escape so he jumped out the window, then he fell in a bush. He went in the road, he tried to destroy a car, but he couldn't do it, so he gave up. He went in the middle of the road. Then he tried to open the door then tried again and again and climbed up the wall up the stairs, opened the door and saw his friends on the bench. So he said, "Where are you?"
They all came running to him saying, "You're back finally."

Harry McLean (7)
Marden Lodge Primary School, Caterham

The Royal Battle

"I want to go to our base," said the lazy guard.
"No because it's been destroyed by the aliens."
"Why?" asked the lazy guard. "Let's go to the doll's house."
"Okay, only if you stop being lazy, okay?"
They got to the doll's house, then they found a zombie in the darkness. They both hid in the bedroom. He had one more bomb. Tony ran as fast as he could and *kaboom!* Tony went to the battleground and went to battle again.

Noah Lukasz Latter (9)
Marden Lodge Primary School, Caterham

The Adventure Of The Dangerous Blender

Once upon a time, there was a little Lego police guy, who'd been moving around the house when his owner was gone.

He played in the kitchen, then suddenly he saw this big machine with a blade. So then he climbed until he reached the top of the dangerous blender.

When the Lego police guy made it to the top, he slipped and fell down into the dangerous blender. He tried to escape but failed badly.

Then his owner came back from work. He caught the Lego police guy moving about in the blender. Now he knows what Legos do.

Karl Carreon (9)

Marden Lodge Primary School, Caterham

The Silly Arrow

The arrow got dropped once and he got left there for a while. Then he finally woke up, it took him a while to wake up but he did it. He got out through a short cut. The human saw him but he pretended, he got away with it. The arrow saw the board. The board said, "Not you again."
"Yes me!" said the arrow. He kept jumping on the board. So he broke his leg. the arrow's surgery came and he got wrapped up like a mummy. When he sneezed, he fell to the floor. He said, "Ouch! Ouch!"

Daisy Terry Santos (7)
Marden Lodge Primary School, Caterham

Alex The Racer

Alex was just relaxing and then he saw a new person who was a driver, and he wanted to race. So he went to him and asked if he could race. He said, "Sure!" So then they made a bet, and started the race, in three, two and one and they were off. He started to hit Alex's toy car and then went full speed and wherever he went there would be fire. Then his engine went off and Alex was in the lead, and he went down the hill and he won and he got a congratulatory trophy.

Kieran Wamukulu (8)
Marden Lodge Primary School, Caterham

Footballer

One day, there was a little figure called Mitchell. The toy worked by itself. It was the best but he was not good at football, and so he was trying to be the best, and he got a lot better. Later at football he was a freestyler, they do all the tricks. He watched his phone until he could do the best tricks and keep getting better. So he pushed himself to the limit. Finally, he was the third best footballer in the world. He trained and trained, and he became the best.

Mitchell Brown (9)
Marden Lodge Primary School, Caterham

Untitled

Once upon a time, there was a playdoh man called Johndoh who got stuck in a box with his friends called Woody and Rexy, who were going to get sold to charity. But they didn't want to leave their owner, so they tried to escape, but the indestructible box was too heavy to tip over. So they tried to cut it open with teeth, but it did not work. So they all pushed and opened it and lived happily ever after.

Nicolei James Roberts (9)
Marden Lodge Primary School, Caterham

Toy Story

"Master, the soldiers have scoured the area, the coast is clear."

"Before we escape we need all of the toys to gather up to tell them the plan to escape. First, we need to get the key for the door, second, we need to use the key on the door to get outside and escape."

"Got it, got it Master."

"Now unlock the door. I have now escaped."

We escaped.

Caiden Chapman (8)
Marden Lodge Primary School, Caterham

The Great Brutus Bake-Off!

"Oh no, we've forgotten the cake!" cried Mum.
"Oh well," replied Dad tiredly, "I'll buy one tomorrow."
With that they both went to bed. They didn't notice a little furry creature was looking concerned in the shadows. Quick as a flash, Brutus (Ellie's favourite cuddly Alsatian puppy) rounded up the troops and sped downstairs to the kitchen. Together, the army and Sylvanian families set to work. Were there enough eggs?
The alarm went. Ellie woke up and rolled over to see Brutus with thick, dark chocolate smeared around his velvety muzzle. How strange!
Happy birthday my lovely Ellie, thought Brutus.

Eleanor Jowett (8)
Meath Green Junior School, Horley

The Lost Elephant

Humphrey the elephant was Chloe's favourite teddy. Humphrey was very lucky, he got to go to Santa's grotto with Chloe. He got left by Chloe inside Santa's grotto. Humphrey was lying on the floor when Shorty the elf noticed someone had left him behind. Shorty scooped Humphrey up and took him to Santa's workshop to show him where the magic of Christmas happens. Humphrey was mesmerised by all the lights, snow, presents and toys in the workshop, but all Humphrey wanted was to get home to Chloe. Santa loaded his sleigh with presents and Humphrey and headed to Chloe's.

Chloe Kirby (8)
Meath Green Junior School, Horley

Food For Everyone

"Wake up, wake up everyone, wake up!" shouted Bear. "Let's go and get some food."
They crept across the room and down the stairs, into the kitchen and to the fridge. Climbing on top of each other's shoulders, they opened the fridge and got loads of food. Once one toy had got food, they would go underneath the bottom toy's legs and it would carry on like that. When everyone had got food, they quickly, but quietly, climbed the stairs... They had the food, but one hour later they all had food left. A person lurked towards them slowly...

Rebecca Markan (9)
Meath Green Junior School, Horley

A Little Adventure!

Once upon a time, Owl was bored and he wanted someone to play with so he decided to get out of the letterbox to explore. Owl came across a river and couldn't get across. Owl fell into a dirty ditch next to the river and was stuck. Close by was a rabbit.

"Help! Help!" yelled Owl. "I am stuck."

The rabbit turned around, "Oh hello there, what is the matter?" said the rabbit.

"I got stuck in this hole and I can't get out."

Rabbit helped Owl out and Owl made his way home. Safe and sound Owl was indeed!

Jaimee Greeno (8)

Meath Green Junior School, Horley

The Mystic Game

In the bedroom was a stuffed teddy bear named Poliwag. It was dark in the bedroom. Poliwag took a stride towards the door. Quickly Poliwag hid. Just then the door opened. A little girl named Angelina walked in and got into bed and slept. The door was still open so Poliwag ran for the door. Poliwag slept.

When Poliwag awoke, she found herself in a video game. Poliwag walked forward. After she completed the tenth level she came across a monster, it was an ugly monster. After many tries Poliwag eventually defeated the monster. Poliwag found it was a dream.

Angelina Wenn (9)
Meath Green Junior School, Horley

Millie The Mouse

"Wheee!" screamed Millie the Mouse as she was jumping on the trampoline. Suddenly, she saw something up in the tall, leafy tree that fell out. She was worried because she thought that the animal would eat her up, so she scrambled out of the trampoline and rushed to the garden door and went inside. When she got inside she remembered that she was supposed to stay outside because the owner was having a party for the night, so she had to rush to her house without being seen by other people. When she got back home she said, "Phew!"

Ellie Jones (7)
Meath Green Junior School, Horley

Flash Hurts His Paw

Carina went to her cosy bed. As soon as Carina went to sleep, Flash got out of bed and started to run around. "Ow!" said Flash the chocolate Labrador. The other toys came over to see what had happened. Flash had badly hurt his small broken paw. Flash had stepped on a small figure. Flash was so badly hurt he had to snuggle up with Carina instead of crazily playing around with the other toys or filling up the bath with lots of cold water and bubbles. Flash couldn't get to sleep because the ducks were quacking so incredibly loudly.

Carina Sophie Card (8)
Meath Green Junior School, Horley

Teddy And Me

Once upon a time, there lived a girl, Beatrix, and her teddy called Rainbow. Rainbow and Beatrix were at home. On that day, Beatrix went to the airport. At the airport they had some lunch and had to go and get on a plane. They were going on holiday. But 30 seconds later, the bear, Rainbow, went missing. Beatrix was so upset because their plane was going to leave without them. When the girl got home after being in America for two weeks, they had to go to bed. Meanwhile, her mum and dad found Rainbow.

Beatrix Smith (9)
Meath Green Junior School, Horley

The Hungry Sheep

Once upon a time, there was a little toy sheep called Sarah. Sarah was a little bit greedy too. She felt like eating some pie. Sarah was starving! So, as quietly as possible, she crept down the uneven steps, which led her to the kitchen. Suddenly, a tabby cat approached the innocent little sheep. Sarah made a run for it! The tabby chased her around the house, because she thought Sarah was a big ball of wool! Thankfully, the girl spotted them chasing each other, so she got out some pie and shared it all together.

Esme Sophia Austin (9)
Meath Green Junior School, Horley

Little Ted And Elliot

One day, Little Ted was put on the wrong shelf and ended up with the big teddies. They bullied him all the time because of his size. Then one day, an elephant was put next to Little Ted. The next day, the big teddies were bullying Little Ted. Then, to the big teddies' surprise, Elephant helped Little Ted to escape. Then, one day, a lady bought them both for a friend of her's baby and he loved them. After nine years he still loves them. So that's why he is sitting at his table now, writing about his toys.

Elliot James Denyer (9)
Meath Green Junior School, Horley

Mr Snugls

In 1940 there was a toy dog called Mr Snugls. He was in charge of the canines but he got trapped in a boat for two months. He had nothing to do, but the battle went on for two months. All the food got taken, he was starved. Just after the battle he got food.

They found out that he needed to get to the vet to re-stuff him. He had surgery. It was stressful. Luckily, it was successful. He was better and he got a big cuddle.

"I'm glad you're back!" and he got given a silver medal.

Joshua Ryan Card (8)

Meath Green Junior School, Horley

Scotty's Big Adventure

I was asleep when Scotty the toy dog crept out of the room and went on an adventure. When I woke up, Scotty was gone. I looked everywhere but I could not find him. The next night, I watched out for Scotty. I saw him, so I followed him and he led me under the sea. I saw fish, sharks and so on. We had to finally decide to go back up because it was morning and Mum would be angry if we weren't home. So we went up and got back, that was the best!

Phoebe Dupres (7)

Meath Green Junior School, Horley

Bob And The Putty Tin

"Done!" Lucy said as she tied the knot in her toy that she was making.

"What is he called?" asked Mum.

"Bob!" Lucy replied.

At eight o'clock Bob came to life.

"Oh! Wait, I can talk, wait, I'm talking!" said Bob. "One, two, three."

Bob turned around and saw a dinosaur counting his steps! "Argh!" screamed Bob, as he stepped into a putty tin.

Lucy entered the room, saw Bob covered in putty and yelled, "Mum!" before swinging him in the wash. With her mum beside her, they watched Bob get clean. *Wish! Wash! Swish! Swash!* Bob was clean, hooray!

Hannah Lee (9)
Reigate Priory Junior School, Reigate

Dreaming Or Not Dreaming?

There Josh was, sitting at his old wooden table, playing his brand-new game. He was sure of it. But then, all of a sudden he was lying on the floor, unconscious, weary-eyed with a throbbing headache. He didn't know when it had happened or why it had happened, all he knew was that he was definitely on the floor. Josh gradually stood up, but then, without doubt, fell back down again, because what he had seen right before his little eyes, was a board game playing itself. Was it happening or was he actually dreaming without knowing?

Naomi Saunders (10)
Reigate Priory Junior School, Reigate

Skylanders Stop

"Bye!" yelled Liam as he left the house.

As soon as Liam left the house, Glowground came to life.

"Argh!" he sighed. "C'mon YouTube and Boiler!" he yelled.

"Nooo!" they exclaimed.

"Wanna party?" Glowground asked.

"Wheee! Woah!" they yelled as they got absorbed into the light.

"Yes!" YouTube yelled.

"Party on the dance floor!" Boiler announced.

"Hello!" Liam yelled.

"Freeze!" Glowground yelled as they partied.

"Whaaat?" announced Liam. "Stop it Brain!" Liam yelled.

"One quarter star! That game is playing with my mind!'

"Wheee!" sighed Glowground. "It's good, we didn't get found!"

Liam McKay (7)
St Martin's CE (A) Junior School, Epsom

The Pilot Who Survived

Hi, my name is Googly, let me tell you about this epic journey. Come see my new friend, I'm telling them about the plane journey.

"Not that one again!" groaned Big Underpants.

"Where's the parts?"

"They're right under my bed."

"Well get them."

"Right away Sir."

"Freeze, John's coming."

"Phew, that was close."

One by one, they got the pieces. "Rear engine - check, wing one - check and wing two - check. Tail - check. Fire exits - check."

"Can we have a break?"

"Yes."

"Footmen."

"Argh!" John's enormous foot crushed all of them except from one - the survivor. He flew the plane.

Leander Anselm William Law (8)

St Martin's CE (A) Junior School, Epsom

The Emergence Of Mary Poppins

Click! All the lights were off. Out of the darkness came an unusual muffled squeak from Mary Poppins. The cupboard doors flew open and Mary Poppins crawled cautiously out.

"Are you alright?" asked a plump stuffed dog.

"O'course," giggled Mary Poppins.

"Yawn!" a small creak came from the bed.

"Who are you anyway?" asked the stuffed dog.

"Mary Poppins!" answered Mary Poppins nervously. "I'm new!"

Mary Poppins went over to the stuffed dog. The stuffed dog snuggled her. "Milo's up to mischief again. Is anyone brave enough to drive him back?" asked the stuffed dog.

"I'll do it!" exclaimed Mary.

Seraphina Lucy Hastings (7)

St Martin's CE (A) Junior School, Epsom

Zaptos Vs Bentos Destructor

Zaptos loves fighting Bentos Destructor! On the night of 5th November (during the fireworks) they hid inside the haunted mansion. Zaptos was frightened but Bentos was brave. These two characters are actually action figures who have come alive! *Pow, pop, bang!* The fireworks began. Zaptos jumped out of his skin and Bentos took this chance to karate slam him. He fell and froze with fear. Bentos Destructor then power punched Zaptos and Zaptos flew into his owner's bedroom. Jeff (Zaptos' owner) saw Zaptos shaking and realised he was alive! Bentos Destructor lived on happily knowing he'd defeated Zaptos. Hooray!

Benart Hoti (8)

St Martin's CE (A) Junior School, Epsom

The Big Battle

One night, when everyone was asleep, a Pokémon card started moving. All of the other cards began to walk towards the portal. Immediately they were transported to a battle arena. They started to battle. The first round was Magikarp vs Rayquaza. Magikarp defeated Rayquaza by using splash. The next round was Charizard vs Venasaur. Charizard defeated Venasaur by using flamethrower. The final round was Steelix vs Nidoking. Steelix used bind. Nidoking used double kick. The match ended in a draw.

Just then, Edward woke up and sent the arena flying through the air. Edward destroyed the arena and the cards.

Jion Park (8)

St Martin's CE (A) Junior School, Epsom

Mission Super Toys!

"Good evening Cowboy Guff," whispered Mr Twinkletoes, the toy cat.
"No time for dawdling," said Guff impatiently.
"You've got a slot in New Zealand for a girl called Mina."
"Roger that Guff!"
Suddenly the window flew open and Mr Twinkletoes clambered into a brightly-coloured hot-air balloon sparkling in the moonlight. He recorded his directions on the toytulator and in the click of his claws he was speeding off to New Zealand.
Thump! He landed in Mina's bedroom.
As the sun rose, Mina awoke and the hot-air balloon was just a shimmering, shooting star.

Lilly Lambert (8)
St Martin's CE (A) Junior School, Epsom

Monkey Mission!

Once upon a time, there were some monkeys who wanted to go to the window and escape. The chief monkey had a loud booming voice.

One of the monkeys had an idea, "We could go under the blanket over there?" suggested Fluffy.

"Yes, good idea," responded the chief.

So they all crept towards the blanket. Suddenly, the boasting pig emerged from the dust.

"Going to escape? Well you won't!" boomed the pig.

The pig forced them to go back. They were really unhappy. Luckily, they found some popcorn and went to sleep with full tummies and happy hearts.

Elle Watts (7)
St Martin's CE (A) Junior School, Epsom

Fluttershy

Once upon a time, there was a toy named Fluttershy. She had lots of friends. When I wasn't around Fluttershy had her own life. She could talk, walk, sing and Fluttershy loved to play hide-and-seek. She would play with her friends but sometimes she got sad because her best friend had gone away.

On a bright, sunny morning Fluttershy's best friend, Rainbow Dash came back. They played together and brushed each other's hair and made beautiful gowns.

Now I feel happy because Fluttershy's best friend is back and when I'm not there I know they are both happy!

Ayat Irfan Ashraf (7)

St Martin's CE (A) Junior School, Epsom

Funny Bunny's Funky Street Adventure

One day, Abigail packed her bag for school. Funny Bunny waited for the car to leave. Abigail left! Funny Bunny came to life. He hopped around her bedroom. He opened her 'All About Me' book, lifted the tab and took out her medals. Funny Bunny leapt out the window and onto the street. He danced with Abigail's medals. Suddenly, a car went zooming past. Emily and Mummy were home to get ready for a party.

Emily said, "Pretty bunny!"

Funny Bunny leapt up into Abigail's bedroom and as Mummy came in he became lifeless. Abigail arrived home and knew nothing.

Abigail Wilson (8)
St Martin's CE (A) Junior School, Epsom

Big Bear's Big Surprise!

Everyone's at Granny's house. Big Bear wakes up and puts on Finlay's Manchester United kit. He goes outside to practise his skills but the ball goes over the fence. Big Bear asks Marcus Marmotte to collect the ball and he agrees. The ball comes back but another ball flies over. A face peers over the fence and the toys fall over.

A boy says, "Finlay is strange, he must be mad!" As soon as he cannot be seen, Big Bear goes back inside. In Finlay's bedroom he hears a mysterious voice saying, "You have just been scouted for Manchester United!"

Finlay Cantwell (8)
St Martin's CE (A) Junior School, Epsom

Nooshy Pig, Squeezing Gorilla And The Rubik's Cube

One day, Freddie was at school. Nooshy Pig and Squeezing Gorilla wanted to solve a Rubik's cube, so they left Nooshy World and visited Freddie's house.

"Come on, let's find his Rubik's cube," said Squeezing Gorilla.

"I've found two," replied Nooshy Pig.

So they played with it. They couldn't figure out how to solve it, so they watched a YouTube tutorial.

Halfway through, Freddie came home, so they ran and jumped into Nooshy World.

Nooshy Pig announced, "We're safe," with a sigh of relief!

Freddie Oberon Smith (7)
St Martin's CE (A) Junior School, Epsom

Untitled

The children all leave for school and the parents go out for breakfast. The toy rabbit sneaks out into the garden.

She hesitates, "Shall I bring a friend? I will, I'll bring my friend, Bear." So instantly she jumps up and runs to Bear. "Come, let's go and play."

They dig holes and have lots of fun. But the gardener arrives. Rabbit tries to escape but she's stuck in a weed. Bear can't help so they both remain still. The gardener lifts them up. He leaves them on a branch and then returns them to the children. They're so pleased.

Isla Ashong Barton (8)

St Martin's CE (A) Junior School, Epsom

Lollie's Adventure

Lollie dashed from side to side as Dusty yawned lazily. Pippa said, "Why don't we go on an adventure?" so off they went.

Whilst they were walking, a dash of red and black flashed past them. Pippa touched it. It took them back in time, and before they knew it they were back in the little girl's room all warm. Then the door bell rang and the little girl stepped in followed by two bigger people.

Quickly they froze as the little girl picked them up and cried, "Daddy, these toys are moving. I don't want them anymore!"

Lula Rose Bloom (7)

St Martin's CE (A) Junior School, Epsom

The Teddy Who Willed For A Friend!

Once upon a time, there lived a pink teddy who willed for a friend. So one morning he got up, cleaned his teeth and went into the woods to hunt for a friend. By a tree he met a toy badger who had a splinter in his paw.

"Would you like some help?" said the bear.

"Yes, yes, yes please," said the badger.

So the bear very gently pulled out the splinter.

"You're a very good friend, would you like to be my friend?" said the badger.

And they were friends forever and they lived nicely and happily.

Rosie Anne Martin (8)

St Martin's CE (A) Junior School, Epsom

The Purple, Jumping Bunny

The purple bunny wakes up and yawns. She immediately pushes the doors open. She starts to stroll out and a bear is confused. She starts to jump around, knocking everything on its side. The purple bunny hops down the stairs and starts eating every carrot in the kitchen. She was being followed by the bear.

The purple bunny got so mad that she screamed, "You bad bear! You are going to pay for this!" She lost her temper and started to jump so hard that she knocked down the food. She started jumping but this time knocked the house down.

Daisy Mowle (8)

St Martin's CE (A) Junior School, Epsom

The Secret Cat

One night, a small black cat appeared. Nobody saw her, nobody heard her. She crept across my bedroom and took one of my toys, Ava. Ava was very petrified, she couldn't seem to get off the strange, mysterious cat. It brought her to the kitchen. The kitchen seemed eerie to Ava. Ava didn't like it. She ran back to me but the cat just took my other toy, Skipit, and now he has been lost forever. Ava told me all about it the next day. "Skipit!" I cried.

We waited and waited but the mysterious black cat never came back.

Lucy Tilley (8)
St Martin's CE (A) Junior School, Epsom

Freddie The Toy Dog And Kitkat The Cat - Toy Fight

One day, a toy dog, Freddie, tried to pounce on Kitkat. He had a plan to fight and kill Kitkat, so now what would Kitkat do? Freddie decided to creep up on Kitkat, so they started pouncing on each other. They started scratching and biting each other. Now Kitkat hid behind the sofa. Freddie sniffed the lounge but Freddie couldn't find Kitkat so he kept on sniffing. As soon as Freddie was going to give up, he decided to wait and wait for Kitkat. Then he decided to stop. Hannah came in and said, "Freddie, come for a walk."

Tamsyn Dewis (7)
St Martin's CE (A) Junior School, Epsom

The Explorer

Once upon a time, Edward had an amazing amount of Lego. When no humans were around a Lego figure came to life! Suddenly, a giant Lego monster chased Edward so he got in his van and the monster ran after Edward. He drove through a cavern that he could drive through so then the monster ran away, back home. Then they came across a forbidden jungle that had a temple with gems in but a panther was guarding the treasure. Edward snuck inside when the panther was asleep. Edward stole the treasure without the panther realising it was gone.

Edward Cleasby (7)
St Martin's CE (A) Junior School, Epsom

The Lone Russian War Soldier

In World War 4 there was a soldier fighting the Turkish and Mexicans. The one last left alive was in a tank, rushing up the field with just Turkish soldiers. He killed five Turkish men. The man was able to get past the Turkish tanks and grenades were thrown at the tank. He somehow shut down an enemy tank. He got past them then the Mexicans came. He was shot in his legs and his arms, he struggled to stand. Bullets were flying. As grenades flew, a tank shot. The Russian man was killed by Mexican army mines.

Ronan Fowler (7)
St Martin's CE (A) Junior School, Epsom

The Colouring Mission

When Anna was at school the pen box opened slightly and the pens came out. The felt-tip pens peered and saw a colourless Christmas tree so they decided to go on a mission! They wanted to colour it in.

Suddenly, Gold Pen said, "Green Pen, you colour the main tree, Red and Purple, you do the tinsel and I will do the star!"

So they did, but when it was finished they were stuck so Gold Pen tried to save them but nothing happened, so they decided to stay there because the human was coming. Anna looked amazed!

Anna Laura Irene Montagano (8)
St Martin's CE (A) Junior School, Epsom

Baby Santa

Once, there was a baby Santa who was in the North Pole getting Teddy to bring presents to the little children but Santa could not because an army came and there was only 23 hours left and 23 hours is not enough time. He didn't have enough presents for the children and the children wouldn't have a nice Christmas. They wouldn't get presents and they would be sad, but the elves helped Santa and the army went away and Christmas was fixed. The children got presents and they were happy. Christmas was saved!

Aleena Bull (7)
St Martin's CE (A) Junior School, Epsom

TD Bear's Adventure

Once upon a time, there was a bear called TD Bear. He was a very lonely bear. He had no friends, no family and no owners. He was a teddy bear you see and life is hard when you're a teddy bear in a shop called Toys 'R' Us.
One day, a boy came to buy a new teddy bear. TD was excited because the boy was heading his way. TD leapt down from his shelf and looked quite happy. The boy looked down and picked TD up! Now TD wasn't lonely, he was very, very, very, very happy!

Jai Baghdadi (7)
St Martin's CE (A) Junior School, Epsom

Freddie The Lonely Puppy

One dark, stormy day there was an amazing, cute and fluffy toy puppy and nobody knew his name. So one day, he wanted to do something fun, so he ran and ran until he reached a restaurant in an old, frightening town. He gently tapped his paw against the door and then the kind owner of the restaurant opened the door. Freddie was scared and he just ran away. Then the owner just closed the door and Freddie walked up to the person and licked her. Then he walked into the darkness and he stared at them.

Hannah Hodgson (7)
St Martin's CE (A) Junior School, Epsom

The Toy Monkey On An Adventure

The toy monkey on an adventure in the zoo was swinging on the trees, having fun when he heard a bang like a bomb and everything changed. The next day, he woke up and he was in a cage and he was very scared that he would get killed. Then he saw a man with a gun and he was getting in his attack position to get ready to attack. So the monkey whacked his tail on the man and the monkey said, "This adventure keeps on getting better and better!"
They lived happily ever after.

Aaron Myers (8)
St Martin's CE (A) Junior School, Epsom

The DJ Cat Toy

There once was a DJ cat toy which danced all night and danced all day. He had parties with his friends and family. One day his mum was stepped on and was crushed so the DJ cat toy sang a sad song. His dad loved it. Next, the owner (a child called Dylan) asked for another DJ cat toy. Amazingly Dylan brought two more DJ cats and all the DJ cats partied and danced for evermore. Of course Dylan never heard about this because he was working hard at school with Miss Davison and his friends.

Dylan Thackwell (7)
St Martin's CE (A) Junior School, Epsom

The Rich Polar Bear

Once upon a time, there was a toy polar bear who was only a cub and she lived everywhere because she had no home. She travelled and travelled and she found a snowy place to live, there she grew up and had lots of friends, one called Storm, the other called Snow but she didn't know her name. So she went to a competition to be rich and everybody called her Tornado. She won the competition and she was rich and everybody knew her name. Everybody loved her so much.

Grace Stanye (7)
St Martin's CE (A) Junior School, Epsom

Cuddly Toy Came Alive

Once upon a time, there lived a little girl called Twinkle Teo, she was only eight years old. Whenever Twinkle Teo skipped out of her bedroom all of her toys came alive. There was actually a lot of cuddly toys. There was a rabbit, a dog, a fish and a little fluffy cat. The human went out of the bedroom and the toys came alive. They started playing a lot of games like 'it' and Hangman. After, the human was about to walk in so they all ran back where they started.

Teagan White (8)
St Martin's CE (A) Junior School, Epsom

The Video Game

Today, Jack the Lego figure woke up and made his breakfast and went on his computer and saw a new game. Then he bought the game and he went to his loft to get his mouse for the computer. When he went to get the mouse he saw a Nintendo Switch. He saw the game he was loading, so he turned it on and tried it. When he was playing it, the game sucked him in and he got in a car. He was in Mario Kart. He was racing in Bowser's castle and wondered what would happen.

Tom Lyle (7)
St Martin's CE (A) Junior School, Epsom

Teddy Make-Up Mission

One morning, my leopard teddy escaped from my bed and put lots of make-up on herself. She pretended to be a clown but there was a massive problem! It was nearly home time for the owner so she needed to wipe it off.

Suddenly, the door opened. The girl ran upstairs and ran into the room and saw the teddy with make-up on. She screamed and her mum came up and started laughing and the girl started laughing and laughed all day and night but then they got tired.

Annabelle Clouting (7)
St Martin's CE (A) Junior School, Epsom

Party! Party!

When I go to school my toys do something amazing. I have a lot of toys including Olaf, Ella and Winter.

One day, I went to school then one of my toys said, "Coast is clear!" It was Ella. And with that all the toys came out for another party. So Winter got all the food ready and the disco ball but they didn't know that I was coming home early. I came in and they didn't know. I screamed and put them all in the bin!

Rose Annie Crouch (7)

St Martin's CE (A) Junior School, Epsom

The Escape

There was a little girl that woke up in her bed on a sunny morning with her teddy bear called Cupcake. But she had to go to school so she got up and went to school. But Cupcake (who was very cheeky) sneaked outside and climbed up a tree. Now this was a very bad idea because she was not a good climber and because of that Cupcake got stuck in a tree. When the little girl came home Cupcake was still in the tree but finally she found her and they had a tea party.

Annabelle Steiner (8)
St Martin's CE (A) Junior School, Epsom

Fire Escape

Once, there was a box of forgotten toy people and they had slept for over a year, but now this was going to change. One day, one of the people awoke, she found herself in shredded clothes. She tried to wake the others but she couldn't. She was worried because she could smell smoke and she saw a warm glow under her feet. Then she figured out it was fire.

"Argh!" she screamed as loud as she could and then everyone woke up.

Noelle Olivia Louis (8)

St Martin's CE (A) Junior School, Epsom

The Toys Called Rose, Daisy And Poppy

When I was out in town I realised something peculiar. Whilst I was out I knew my toy kittens moved because they were in my toy box and then they were on the front door mat. At first I thought it was my sister who might've moved them quickly but I was wrong, so I have no idea what happened. Besides, I always shut my bedroom door. Anyway, if they did move themselves I doubt anyone would believe me as loads of people say I lie!

Emilie Poole (8)
St Martin's CE (A) Junior School, Epsom

The Computer Game

The colonel turned to his men and said to his men, "We need to fight the West Army tonight. We need to find a battlefield and defeat them."
On the way, they passed the big computer and one of the men stood on a key. It sucked them into an army game and they met the Nots Army. They fought them and they won.
"Hooray!" they said.
Suddenly, the computer blew them out of the game and they were at their base.

George Robert King (7)
St Martin's CE (A) Junior School, Epsom

The Army

My army toys were running under my bed. My Lego ran up the stairs and they had a war. The Lego had bricks so they built a base, it was very big. The army got in the base. The Lego men had a secret bit, the army could not find the Lego men. The army men got their tanks. The Lego men built a wall. The army men got their aeroplanes. The Lego men built a car and drove away. The army men could not find the Lego men.

Harry Elia Vine (7)
St Martin's CE (A) Junior School, Epsom

All The Toys Are Gone

One day, I was playing with my toys and then my mum was telling me it was time for lunch. Then my toys were standing up and they found a vent and a screwdriver. They went and unscrewed the screws on the vent and went in the vent. Then they were free and they were outside of the house. Then I had finished and I went back to my room and they were all gone. I was upset about my toys so instead I watched TV.

Zain Griffiths (8)
St Martin's CE (A) Junior School, Epsom

The Robin Who Plays Mario Galaxy!

When I leave for school my toy Robin comes alive. Then my Robin runs down the stairs. He then opens our playroom door and plays Mario Galaxy for hours and hours and hours. But when I come back he never saves it. When it's time to go to bed I snuggle up in my bed with him and go to sleep.

Edward Lewis (7)
St Martin's CE (A) Junior School, Epsom

The Cat The Mouse Forgot

A karate mouse, the deadly room, cheese.

Sniff, sniff, goes Mousabito. He senses cheese across the room, glowing, beautiful, yellow; the quest begins...

Front flips over cables, wall climbing table legs, heroically leaping from heights, wind in his hair... imaginary dramatic music.

The snakes, the last challenge.

He climbs to the tank, screams and slips through the glass.

Triumphantly he steps to the glorious cheese on his hind legs, flicks the fringe he doesn't have, raises up the gorgeous cheese into the air, kisses it and...

Miaow! Squish! Squeal! Scream! Blood, gore, pain, blood, death! Double dramatic music plays. *Miaow!*

Hugh Carter (10)
St Peter's RC Primary School, Leatherhead

Princess Lola's Adventure

The petite bratty doll's life turned upside down as her best friend, Amelia started to forget about her. Lola watched her friend's room turn into a disgusting mess.

"That's it," the dolly retorted, "I'm gonna escape!"

She tried but it failed. Amelia found Lola lying upon her fluffy magenta rug. Lola felt as if she was endlessly flipping until...

"Argh! Wait, where am I?" Lola cried in a rude, disrespectful voice.

"Where all the weirdos are, well at least that's what you called us."

"Wait a second, we're moving, argh!"

"Oh Mummy, please may I have this pretty dolly?"

Renata Suchocka (10)
St Peter's RC Primary School, Leatherhead

Texting Ted

It suddenly landed there, the thing. An inquisitive bear, Ted, became curious. Slowly, quietly he plodded across the bed; would the thing attack? How would it attack? *Bring!* Ted sprang behind a cushion, his chocolate fur was on end. Then his eyes went green, he jumped off the bed and put Robin's sunglasses on...

"Texting Ted. Text, text, selfie!"

"He's possessed!" said the dinosaur.

"Hypnotised!" said the teddies.

The thing was practically glued to his hands! *Creak!* Here comes Robin. "Drop to the floor. Teddies and all!" *Click!* The thing went off, Robin took it away and Ted was back!

Heidi Owen (10)
St Peter's RC Primary School, Leatherhead

Bo-Bo's Adventure

There was a creak, a sudden movement and out came Bo-Bo with all his little friends, "The coast is clear, go!" he cried.

They stood as still as a brick wall in the strong wind. "Bo-Bo where do we go?" asked Bo-Bo's brother.

"Oh sorry straight ahead to the food!" said Bo-Bo.

When they got there a toy unicorn was eating it.

"Oi, get off our food!" shouted Bo-Bo.

"Your food? This is mine!" the unicorn shouted.

"Wow, the human!" Bo-Bo said.

"Where?" asked Unicorn.

"Ha! Your food is gone," Bo-Bo laughed.

"This isn't the end!" said the unicorn.

Zoe Tubb (11)
St Peter's RC Primary School, Leatherhead

Santa's Visit

Bang! Santa fell. "What was that?" questioned Teddy peeking out of the toy box. Before him was a man in red and white. "There's a man, he's an intruder!" he cried.

"Attack!" blurted Sergeant Sammy. They all jumped out, even soldiers One and Two. "Fire!" screamed Sergeant Sammy.

Santa turned slowly, but before he could take another step, a pin shot into his bottom. "Argh!" Santa yelled.

"Got him!" shouted Teddy.

Santa limply fell to the floor. "Awww!" he screamed in agony.

Lots of noise was made. Jimmy opened an eye as Santa disappeared, leaving him exciting presents.

Aidan Hindle (10)

St Peter's RC Primary School, Leatherhead

146

A Bad Piggy Comes To Town!

Pretend you're not in your world, you're in a toys' world and you're a toy too.

"Why have you all grown? Bobba? Is that you?"

You're covered by an orange blanket, "What... what's happening, Jim, the teddy, Bobba?"

Voices are scattered around.

"Where am I?" A small light blinds you.

"Keep quiet, I'm just gonna ask you a few questions... Do you wanna die?"

His slang voice intimidates you, the only option is to make a run for it. "I... I..."

You launch yourself off the chair, Bobba pulls your arm. *Nee noor, plop!* No arm, no head, run!

Lucy Alya Mitchell (10)

St Peter's RC Primary School, Leatherhead

Lucky Escape

"Let's go," whispered Fred. Jim started the engine.
Fred was on top of the small toy camouflaged
tank. Tim was downstairs. Now was their chance.
Everyone was relying on them to get the big,
yummy biscuit. The wheels started moving,
everyone was nervous. The door was open. They
took a deep breath and went through a whole new
world. One problem, huge, scary stairs.
"Let's go," Jim murmured. Then... "Ouch, ouch!"
They looked outside, no more stairs.
"What?" Tim shouted. He took them outside and
started playing. "Oops!" He lost control. They
started hurtling towards the giant tree...

Joe Pisa (10)
St Peter's RC Primary School, Leatherhead

The Broken Teddy Bear

Bash, boom! I enter the fire-breathing rocket. Andy lifts me up and the wind sweeps me off his hand. I drift into my neighbour's unfamiliar garden. *Oh no!* I think, *Andy said there'd be a hurricane soon!* A weak gust of wind pushes me up onto the fence. Night comes quickly, butterflies urge into my cotton-filled stomach... *Crash!* I zoom into the air until I float; it is dark.

"Where am I? I miss Andy." Cotton-like tears roll down my cheek.

"Teddy, Teddy!" Andy shouts. His alarm screams... *Poof!*

"I'm not stuffed anymore, Andy come save me..."

Lucy Bond Rodriguez (10)

St Peter's RC Primary School, Leatherhead

One Brave Knight Lost Under The Dreaded Bed...

"I'm lost," sighed Dave all because giant, glowing, green shapes started to appear all around him...
"Who are you?" they murmured, as if possessed.
"You're an invader!"
"Attack!"
The aliens walked slowly towards Dave. Eventually they lifted him, carrying him into the corner.
Two hours later, an army of aliens emerged, licking their lips as if about to eat him, muttering something that sounded like 'the claw', then he saw what they were talking about - a massive grabber in a box with foam. They were ready to pick him up, but he ran for his life!

Ben Fry (10)
St Peter's RC Primary School, Leatherhead

The Mysterious Figure

"I can't do it!" This sergeant was experiencing war. "I must end this war even if I die!"

"Well you can," said a mysterious figure, "if you cross the most dangerous ocean ever; Lethal Endless Giant Ocean, or Lego for short."

He decided to cross the ocean. It was very harsh and it resulted in many injuries but he finally made it.

"I've been expecting you!" Someone was already there. "I told you about this place so I could test my powers. I am Time Lord."

"No!" The sergeant punched him and he died. A clock exploded. The war ended.

Dylan Trousdale (11)
St Peter's RC Primary School, Leatherhead

A Christmas Mix-Up

A present tore open, a robot dog popped out.
"Where am I?" it called.
"Hello, you must be the new toy, there's one every year on Christmas because our owner asks for a new toy from Santa every year," said a toy bear.
"Mommy, Daddy, it's Christmas!" came a voice.
"Quick get back in the box, our owner can't know we're alive!" said Bear.
The child opened the present and a frown tore across his face. "I didn't want this for Christmas!" the child said, then ran to his room.
"Santa must have got mixed up!" said a toy elf.

Nathan Van Niekerk (11)
St Peter's RC Primary School, Leatherhead

The Army's Great Escape

"The coast is clear! Run"

Troop 67 toy soldiers ran for cover behind Cameron's toy box. The teddy bears were clambering down from the bed one by one, and marching towards them.

"Steady your guns!"

Gunshots were firing and toys ran across the carpet. Sargent Sam blew his whistle and in ran Buzz the labrador. "Get on!" barked Buzz hurriedly. Once they were all on, Buzz ran out of the room and flew straight into Cameron! He laughed happily and stroked Buzz. "What have you been up to, you silly dog?"

You'll never know what your toys get up to!

William Ralph (10)

St Peter's RC Primary School, Leatherhead

Crash!

Spinning and whirling in the air the army helicopter zoomed about. "This is fun!" cried a little happy boy. "Uh-oh!"

The army people inside pressed the emergency button. "Tree ahead, land now!" they screamed, but it was too late... *Crash!* The helicopter had flown into some evil branches that grabbed onto the toy.

Sadly, Bobby had to go in for bed. In the frightening night, the army men got out of their helicopter, the branches swayed wearily, whispering sad thoughts. They heaved the helicopter up and revved the engine, flying out of the branches and into their cosy bedroom.

Quinn Pinkerton (10)
St Peter's RC Primary School, Leatherhead

Mission Impossible: Race To The Sausage

The door slammed shut. Lights clicked off. It was time. Unimouse awoke. They had been glued together by Bill, their owner. The mouse part smelt a wisp of sausage. So their quest to eat began. They ran speedily, scuttling across Bill's messy room. They managed to escape. Then, they faced the biggest challenge of them all; the stairs. Soldiers were spotted, they too had escaped. They gave Unimouse parachutes. They flew down like baby birds. They landed with a thud. They found a meal. They went for a bite then *squish, squeal*, blood... Death. The dog viciously pounced, slaughtering them.

Dave Meinson Babu (10)
St Peter's RC Primary School, Leatherhead

Hide-And-Seek

"Fifty! I'm coming!" and then once she had counted... Flavia ran into the Chinese doll house. She was finding her twin, Rana. She searched and searched until... What? She heard the sound of music. She ran as fast as she was able. She followed it into the garden. When she went outside she saw a party.

"Found you!" Flavia cried and then she ran into her sister, crashing into the buffet. After his happened, the unicorn with the cold heart arrived... *Snap!* Everyone turned - she was there holding a camera recording everything they did.

Emily-Mae Jackson (10)

St Peter's RC Primary School, Leatherhead

The Fear Of Bob Piglet

My name's Bob, Bob Piglet. It's been my name since I malfunctioned in Toys 'R' Us. Don't get it twisted, I love my owner, I only worry about his baby brother. Once, he tore off part of my ear. It was incredibly painful, but the thing was I had to stay completely still. I've tried to escape through the vent, but I was too fat and couldn't fit through (I really need to lower my large Lego brick diet). I hear footsteps. It must be my owner coming to play with me. I'll have to stop writing.
Dribble.
"Argh!"

Finlay Kelly (10)
St Peter's RC Primary School, Leatherhead

The Magnificent Magician

The ghastly pirate and his fighting toy ship roamed the water. The cruise ship on a luxurious cruise moved through the red sea. The pirate ship saw the cruise ship and said, "At last, some intruders!" The magnificent magician saw and alerted the captain. The pirate fired a bullet and kept on firing. The magician swam across to the boat and jumped aboard. He used his magic to try and capture him but eventually he got the pirate. "Yes!" the magician said. He put him in the prison on board and went to grab a delicious, tasty doughnut.

Jack Robinson (10)
St Peter's RC Primary School, Leatherhead

The Secretive Toys

One day, a boy called Ray who was six years old walked back from home in a hurry. He opened the door, put his bag away and quickly ran upstairs. Then he eventually unlocked his box of toys and played with them for hours.

Suddenly, his mum shouted, "Tea!"

"Coming!" Ray shouted back. He flicked his light, but heard a fall, he looked back and Steve was on the floor (his toy).

Ray picked up Steve, then Steve shouted, "Now!" Suddenly, all of the toys he owned came out of the box and pinned him to the ground...

Dan Cowling (11)

St Peter's RC Primary School, Leatherhead

The Dusty Antique

There was once an old rocking horse and a lonely child. They were the best of friends. They were very similar too. They both had lovely golden hair. But things started to change. Boxes were lying around and everyone was excited and stressed and rushing around. One day they left. No one visited the poor palomino rocking pony until one sad day a very modern family moved in. They spent a lot of time installing their new kitchen before they saw the dusty antique. That fateful day they picked up the poor horse and threw him in the smelly skip.

Molly Ellen Serdet (11)
St Peter's RC Primary School, Leatherhead

The Nutella-Eating Elf

Elfie flew across the room, trying to scavenge for food. He hunted for the Nutella on the top of the shelf reserved for his owner, Maddie. He grabbed a spoon out of the cupboard and ripped off the plastic and dipped the spoon in the Nutella, he ate a whole spoonful of it. The owner, Maddie, woke up from a nightmare and walked downstairs, putting her pink nightdress on. Walking downstairs, she walked towards the kitchen and was too tired to notice that he was hiding in the fridge.

"Santa, I didn't blow my mission!"

Maddie Ciesco (10)

St Peter's RC Primary School, Leatherhead

Norcuni's Small Adventure

Bobby walked into Norcuni the unicorn's room and shrank him with a shrink gun. Norcuni then set off on his small adventure to grow back to normal. He charged off the bed. Then he realised this would be hard. His first challenge was Lego. He had to climb mountains of it. He finished and was not ready for what would happen next... He had to make a long run with no food or water. He knew he would not have either for a long time. His instinct told him one thing: just keep going. He failed and starved while running.

Thomas Robin de Schulthess (10)
St Peter's RC Primary School, Leatherhead

The Bone!

It was right there; Pixie's bone. Fergus was a Lego dog from a set with a white bone, but Zoe had lost the pieces to it. Fergus slowly moved his plastic pieces until he was moving forward. Suddenly Pixie, Zoe's real dog, ran towards Fergus and pushed him over, smashing him into a million tiny Lego pieces. At that moment Zoe turned into the room immediately realising what had happened. She scooped up the pieces and sat down at her desk and got to work. A while later, Fergus was back to normal with a white bone by his side.

Ella Yolande Ferguson (10)

St Peter's RC Primary School, Leatherhead

A New Visitor

Boom! I board the plane and he lifts me up, sweeping me up in the air. Blocks topple over me like an avalanche. A deafening noise hits my ear and he drops me on the floor... Opening my eyes, everything is empty. I stand up and search the whole house. Suddenly, a tall shadow appears in front of my eyes. A vicious child runs into the room, picking me up and dribbling on me. After suffocating me several times in his mouth, he puts me in the washing machine. Unable to hold any strength, I come to an end. *Poof!*

Hannah Cortez (10)
St Peter's RC Primary School, Leatherhead

The Last One

In Devon, a base camp was made by General Tom Smith, he put Sergeant Lee in charge. Sergeant Lee was very bossy when he was angry but I didn't mind. While we were training we could feel the ground shaking. There was an earthquake, but it wasn't; it was the huge titanium and powerful robot. We were not ready, what could we do? We went and got our guns, but it was too late, most of us were wounded, ouch! There was only one left; a sniper, so he fought the robot but that didn't work, so he ran away.

Alex Hollingworth (11)
St Peter's RC Primary School, Leatherhead

Super Subaru

3, 2, 1, *whoosh!* I turned small and got in my Subaru. My brother was outside. He picked up the remote and I started doing doughnuts round my room. *Crash!* I started going down the stairs and it was like a roller coaster for me in the small car. I lost control and a wheel smacked into the stair gate. *Crash!* It was broken. A dog came out of the gloom and the darkness. I started spinning round and round. Paddy started to bark. I stopped. Arlo came in and picked me up...

Max Murray (11)

St Peter's RC Primary School, Leatherhead

The Robot Who Was Not Loved

Rob was a lonely robot that no one ever played with. Rob had been there for years. No one ever took interest in him, the issue was he was a faulty toy. One afternoon, Rob escaped the toy store and ended up in a completely different store. But it was an antiques shop. Rob felt confused but he started exploring the uncharted territory. Eventually Rob found a tall desk where a sad man was working on a new toy.

Rob came up to the man and said, "Hello, can you fix me?" and so the man did.

Matías Iglesias Iglesias (10)
St Peter's RC Primary School, Leatherhead

The Night I Met My Old Friend

I woke up to a bang on the roof and a, "Ho, ho, ho!" I quickly ran to the kitchen, scavenging for food and I found some Choco-Bons. After one hour of hiding and eating so much, I slightly opened the door to the room I'd been hiding in and ran to the Christmas tree. I was suddenly stopped and I saw a black, dirty boot. I then looked up slowly and saw a red pair of trousers. I looked up again so far I was struggling to breathe and I couldn't believe what I saw... It was Santa.

Alfie Grimley (11)
St Peter's RC Primary School, Leatherhead

The Reindeer Who Climbs The Bed

As the reindeer sat on the edge of the bed, he fell with a knock and, *thump!* He just fell off the bed. He trotted to the end of the bed. He climbed on the box and then onto the mini pool table. Then he thought of the small gap in the bed which led to Tim's feet. He scampered through the gap and he woke up Tim. He grabbed the reindeer and gave him a big hug. Then he went to sleep with him by his head.

Alfie Bowers (11)
St Peter's RC Primary School, Leatherhead

Teddies Vs Toys

"Barbie, where are you? Barbie where are you?" called Tedsta the teddy.

Then, all of a sudden, Tedsta heard a shriek of delight and he saw Barbie flying around with Superman.

"Put her down!" shouted Tedsta.

"Why?" answered Superman.

"Because she's my girlfriend!" called Tedsta.

"Oh really!" said Superman leaning forward and giving Barbie a kiss.

By now lots of teddies and toys had come to look.

"Right, we're declaring war on you!" screamed Tedsta and there was a roar of approval.

The war lasted a long time but in the end the teddies won and Barbie was Tedsta's again.

Thomas Jerrom (10)
Warlingham Park School, Chelsham Common

Teddies Vs Dog

"Let the battle begin!" said Seal.

"Woof, woof!" said Dog.

"Grab the Nerf gun," said Polar Bear.

The teddies started shooting the dog.

The big, ferocious dog jumped on the Nerf gun.

Lateas started throwing toy army men.

The dog snapped at Little Seal. "Argh!" said Little Seal.

Raqwasa threw the dog over. "Thanks Seal."

Just then Octopus had an idea. "Get the sack of really cold peas," said Octopus.

The teddies got the sack of cold peas and threw the peas on the dog.

The dog howled. "Awwww!" howled the dog and ran off.

"We won!" said the teddies.

Rupert Stuart Lee (10)
Warlingham Park School, Chelsham Common

Untitled

"Come on men, we need to run!" said Sergeant Rex. *Crash!* "Oh no, we crashed into a cave and now we are stuck. Good job Buzz!"
Rex and Buzz made a plan, they would rebuild their spacecraft and go back home. Easy right? So that's what they did but then they heard a noise.
"Roar!"
"Who's there?" Buzz said, terrified.
Suddenly Mr Bananahead popped out from the shadows. "Sorry for scaring you. I was sleeping, anyway why are you guys here?"
"Well, Buzz got us crashed, but we are on our way now, bye!"
"See you later."
"Until next time..."

Isobel Haslock (10)
Warlingham Park School, Chelsham Common

Toy Robbery

"We have 18 minutes until the fuzz get here."
Those evil bears at their police station. "Come on
guys, let's go!"
They had already taken out the security guards
and were now in control of the vehicle. "Let's get
this stuff in the Minis."
The Scalextrics accelerated behind the truck.
They started to load up the Minis when a human
saw them but Pete took care of him. Bullets in the
face! More bullets!
"Get the spike balls!" someone cried.
So they took out the cars with the spikes. Finally
everything was done and they escaped. They were
rich!

Jack Norman (10)
Warlingham Park School, Chelsham Common

Raptor's Escape

"How do I get out? I've tried everything!" I roared, clawing and biting at the door. I suddenly realised I could use a coat hanger to lift the lock - it worked! I shot downstairs, wondering how to get home. *I know, I'll turn on the film and jump in the TV.* But I couldn't see the remote. I searched the house until, out the corner of my dinosaur eye, I saw it squished between the sofa cushions! I grabbed it with my raptor claws and selected 'Jurassic Park' - play!

"I'm coming Mum!"

I ran and jumped at the TV. *Crash!*

Conor Maguire (10)
Warlingham Park School, Chelsham Common

A New Home

Tom was with his gran today and he got a new toy robot. He went to play with Robo after football. Gran called, "Teatime!"

"All ready!" Tom went downstairs.

Robo woke up and fell under the bed. He found broken toys. He ran to the garden and hid in the shed. Tom finished tea and headed to his bed but he could not find Robo.

Days went by, still no sign of him. Tom went into the shed to look for the shovel but then he found Robo.

"Wahoo!" Tom shouted. "Look Mum, found him Gran, Mum!"

Caitlin Rose Read Nolan (9)
Warlingham Park School, Chelsham Common

The Piggy Air Force

The piggy air force were sick and tired of hiding from the evil security camera (drone). So one day they decided to take it down! The piggies warned the commander what they were doing and he agreed with the plan. They set up camp and got all the cannons and the piggies were ready to battle. It was the day the piggies took the beast down. The pigs got in formation and then their commander shouted, "Fire!" The pigs were tired. So it was up to me. Then I shot it down and then I was named Champion of Pigs!

Ethan Hardiman (11)
Warlingham Park School, Chelsham Common

Welcome To Games

On Friday 13th January, John Kill and his lads tested their Spitfires. Jonny went in his tank to lead the Spitfires. John Kill and the team were ready to go to London. Jonny got in his tank and started to lead the army cars and the Spitfires. When the lads got to London, they carried their Nerf guns. John Kill shot a person and another person shot him. That gun was a teleporter gun and he travelled to Forza Motorsport 7. He landed in a Nissan GTR in Silverstone. John won the race and was happy. He was trapped!

Jaydon Abban (10)
Warlingham Park School, Chelsham Common

Est.1991

YOUNG WRITERS INFORMATION

We hope you have enjoyed reading this book – and that you will continue to in the coming years.

If you're a young writer who enjoys reading and creative writing, or the parent of an enthusiastic poet or story writer, do visit our website **www.youngwriters.co.uk**. Here you will find free competitions, workshops and games, as well as recommended reads, a poetry glossary and our blog.

If you would like to order further copies of this book, or any of our other titles, then please give us a call or visit **www.youngwriters.co.uk**.

Young Writers
Remus House
Coltsfoot Drive
Peterborough
PE2 9BF
(01733) 890066 / 898110
info@youngwriters.co.uk